Cindy never expected to see Ben again....

"What a wonderfully familiar sight."

At the sound of the strange, deep voice, Cindy jumped, and Star jerked his head up. The greasy hoof-conditioner brush went flying into the bedding, and Cindy spun around to yell at the intruder who had startled them.

She began to snap at the man as she reached out to calm Star. The colt's nostrils flared, and his ears pricked forward as he eyed the stranger. But when Cindy saw the visitor's face, she froze, gaping at the tall, dark-haired man standing in front of Star's stall.

"Ben al-Rihani," she said, hardly able to believe her eyes. "What in the world are you doing here?"

Collect all the books in the Thoroughbred series

THOROUGHBRED Super Editions
Ashleigh's Christmas Miracle
Ashleigh's Diary
Ashleigh's Hope
Ashleigh's Journey

ASHLEIGH'S Thoroughbred Collection
Star of Shadowbrook Farm
The Forgotten Filly
Battlecry Forever!

* coming soon

THOROUGHBRED

CINDY'S DESERT ADVENTURE

CREATED BY
JOANNA CAMPBELL

WRITTEN BY
MARY ANDERSON

HarperEntertainment
An Imprint of HarperCollinsPublishers

HarperEntertainment

An Imprint of HarperCollins*Publishers*
10 East 53rd Street, New York, NY 10022-5299

Produced by 17th Street Productions,
an Alloy Online, Inc., company

HarperCollins books are available at special quantity discounts for bulk
purchases for sales promotions, premiums, or fund-raising.
For information please call or write:
Special Markets Department, HarperCollins Publishers Inc.,
10 East 53rd Street, New York, NY 10022-5299.
Telephone: (212) 207-7528. Fax: (212) 207-7222,

ISBN 0-06-106671-0

Cover art © 2001 by 17th Street Productions,
an Alloy Online, Inc., company

First printing: June 2001

Printed in the United States of America

Visit HarperEntertainment on the World Wide Web at
www.harpercollins.com

❖ 10 9 8 7 6 5 4 3 2 1

*For my friends and neighbors Rachel and Daniel Golda,
and their favorite horse, PF Slick Willie*

"MS. MCLEAN, I'M AFRAID YOU'LL NEVER RACE AGAIN."
The doctor's devastating words echoed in Cindy
McLean's head as she left the downtown Lexington
medical clinic. *Never race again.* Cindy made it out the
door and then leaned against the clinic's rough brick
wall, not trusting her legs to carry her to her car.

An icy gust of January wind swept over her, ruf-
fling her short blond hair. Cindy automatically pulled
her coat closed, feeling a twinge of pain as she shifted
her left shoulder. At least her recent shoulder surgery
had taken care of the constant ache that had tormented
her for the last few years. That was something to be
thankful for, she reminded herself. But at the moment
she didn't feel very grateful.

A group of teenage girls walked by, carrying

brightly colored shopping bags from a downtown department store. Still numb with shock over the doctor's grim words, Cindy listened to them laugh and talk as they crossed the busy street. It seemed strange to see people go on about their business when her life had suddenly been turned upside down.

A second gust of wind sent a scrap of paper tumbling along the sidewalk. It reminded Cindy of the video clip she had watched of one of her more spectacular accidents on the racetrack.

It had been near the end of the Riva Ridge Stakes, and she was galloping her colt into the final stretch, sure they were going to pull off a win. She had eased the Thoroughbred she was riding into a space between the lead horse and the rail. When the outside horse swerved toward her, Cindy's horse slammed into the rail. He flipped, sending her flying into the middle of the track and into the path of the rest of the field of racehorses.

In the video she had looked like a rag doll, rolling and flopping under the churning hooves of the ten Thoroughbreds running that day. She shuddered slightly at the memory and shook her head. But wrecks were what came with racing horses; she knew that. And she was willing to take the risks, if only she could race again.

Another blast of wind cut through her coat, forcing

her to move. Cindy felt like a robot as she walked stiffly to her car. She slid behind the wheel and started the engine to let it warm up. The numbness surrounding her slowly faded, only to be replaced by a terrible, aching emptiness. Cindy clenched her fists and focused on breathing steadily.

Rotator cuff surgery was supposed to have repaired the damage her shoulder had sustained over the years. When Cindy had decided to have the surgery, she had planned to take a few months off to recover, and then return to the track as soon as possible. She had been certain her leave from racing was temporary. But according to the surgeon, repeated abuse had made the joint weak. If she reinjured it, she might never regain full use of her arm. Unless she was willing to take that risk each time she went into the gate, Cindy would never race again.

For the last sixteen years racing Thoroughbreds had been her life. But now any hope that she might return to the track as a jockey had been ripped away with a few words from the surgeon.

A sob caught in her throat, but Cindy gritted her teeth and forced it down. One thing she had learned as a jockey was that if you got knocked down, you got right back up and kept going. The world didn't wait for quitters. And Cindy McLean was no quitter.

Her gaze settled on a sun-bleached parking pass

from Belmont sitting on the dashboard. Cindy had spent the last twelve years at the famous New York track, earning a reputation as one of the best women jockeys, and one of the top all-around jockeys, on the East Coast.

Then, last fall, she had wrenched her shoulder so badly that she had been unable to use it for several weeks. She had forced herself to ignore the pain, but it didn't take long for the trainers and track officials to order her off the track until she had a doctor's clearance.

So Cindy had come home to Whitebrook, the Kentucky breeding and training farm where her father, Ian McLean, worked as the head trainer. As a young orphan who had run away from an unhappy foster home, Cindy had been drawn to Whitebrook by the horses. Ian and Beth McLean had adopted her, and she had grown up working with the Thoroughbreds there, riding and helping to train the high-strung racehorses.

Ashleigh Griffen, a highly acclaimed jockey, owned Whitebrook with her husband, Mike Reese. Ashleigh had helped Cindy fulfill her dream of becoming a jockey. Ashleigh knew how hard a woman had to work to succeed as a jockey, and Cindy had been determined to make Ashleigh proud of her. Cindy sighed. For all her dreams of coming back to Whitebrook a proud success, she sure had been humbled.

4

She put the car into gear and merged with the traffic. It took only a few minutes to get out of downtown Lexington, and soon she was in farm country. She drove past small farms with simple homes and barns, and large estates with long curving drives that led to stately brick mansions and sprawling barns. Rail fences divided rolling fields of Kentucky bluegrass.

Near many of the barns, large paddocks held young Thoroughbreds of every color, from dappled gray to gleaming black. Groups of yearlings stood together, grazing or staging mock battles with each other. Too young to be raced and too old to be with their dams, the colts and fillies would soon be trained to accept the weight of a rider on their backs, and in another year they would begin their racing careers.

At this time of year, most of the broodmares were in the barns or nearby, where they could be closely supervised until their foals were born. Since January 1 was the official birth date of all Thoroughbreds, the mares were bred to foal as close to that date as possible. Then, until the weather warmed up a bit, the mares and foals would be kept inside, warm and safe.

Back in New York, she never saw foals gamboling at their dams' sides, taking those first cautious steps across a paddock. The view from the one window of her apartment was of a brick wall, and the earth in the city was covered with concrete, not lush pasture.

Cindy looked forward to the early spring, when she could see the foals experience the wonder of the outdoors for the first time. That was one good thing about being home, she told herself. When the thought brought a smile to her face, Cindy realized that it was the first time she had smiled all day.

When she reached Whitebrook, Cindy rolled up the gravel drive and past the long white barns that housed Ashleigh and Mike's racehorses. She parked beside the McLeans' cottage. Beth and Ian's car wasn't there, and the house was quiet when she went inside. Her younger brother, Kevin, a senior at Henry Clay High School, wouldn't be home for a few more hours. Beth was probably at the health club where she worked as an aerobics instructor, and Ian was undoubtedly at the barn, helping Ashleigh with the broodmares.

Cindy picked up a stack of mail sitting on the hall table and glanced through it, but there was nothing for her. She thought of the mail that must be piling up at her Elmont, New York, apartment, and cringed. She needed to get up to New York and take care of things there.

At least her racetrack insurance covered all her medical bills, so that wasn't a worry. But disability pay didn't cover her expenses, and she still had the rent and utilities to pay at the apartment. Her savings account was dwindling fast, but she was pretty limited as to what she could do for a job. Not too many people would want to hire a horse trainer with only one good arm. She knew she could ask Ashleigh for a job, but she couldn't be sure if Ashleigh would hire her because she felt obligated or because she really wanted Cindy for the job.

Since she had nothing else to do, Cindy changed into jeans and a sweatshirt, pulled on a warm barn jacket, and headed for Whitebrook's stables. She avoided the broodmare barn. Ashleigh and the Whitebrook staff would be fussing over the expectant mares and newborn foals. Cindy loved to see and handle the foals as much as anyone else, but she knew Ashleigh would ask about her shoulder. Right now Cindy wasn't in the mood to share the bad news. There would be plenty of time later.

Instead she headed for the barn where the racehorses were stabled. Cindy walked by the two empty stalls where Catwink and Raven were normally kept. Naomi Traeger, one of Whitebrook's regular jockeys, was in Florida for the winter racing season with the two fillies. Most of the horses on layoff were in their paddocks for the day, enjoying the clear January weather. Thinking the barn was empty, Cindy started to leave.

But as she headed for the door she heard a familiar whinny. She turned to see a chestnut colt stick his head into the aisle. The colt whinnied again, and Cindy strode down the wide barn aisle toward him.

Wonder's Star nickered softly as she neared, bobbing his nose in her direction. Although Star had a special bond with Ashleigh and Mike's daughter Christina, Cindy had helped nurse the horse while he was recovering from a terrible illness several weeks earlier. Star had helped her remember why she loved Thoroughbreds and racing, and Cindy had developed her own bond with the personable colt.

She picked up a bucket of grooming tools and let herself into Star's stall. The colt nudged her, and Cindy rubbed his sleek neck.

"How are you doing, boy?" she asked. Star craned his neck to sniff at her jacket pockets, but Cindy gently pushed his nose away. "Forget it, greedy," she said shaking her head. "I'm not like Christina. I don't have a pocketful of apple pieces for you. Just a good brushing. But you'll have to put up with a one-armed groom," she added, picking up a soft rubber currycomb. "The doctor said I still need to limit how much I use my left arm for a while." She sighed as she gently massaged his copper-colored shoulder with her good hand. "I'd rather use it grooming you than waste perfectly good time at the physical therapist's office, though."

Cindy eyed Star's flank, nodding in approval as

she noted that the colt had regained almost all the weight and muscle tone he had lost during his illness. "You're looking pretty good, Star," she said. Everyone agreed that the colt had completely recovered, but Christina and Ashleigh were still being cautious about trying to race him too soon after being so sick. Cindy agreed wholeheartedly. If they were even considering racing Star again, they had to take it slowly, letting him build his strength and confidence back day by day.

Cindy grinned wryly. Maybe she should have done the same thing. She should have given herself time to heal before she tried to do too much. Too bad she was only realizing this now, after the damage had already been done.

She worked the currycomb down Star's flank, and the colt lowered his head, blowing out a gusty sigh of contentment.

Cindy felt her worries about her future fade as she groomed the colt. She inhaled Star's sweet scent, mingled with the aroma of the fresh hay, and her tension faded. She picked up a soft polishing brush and crouched down to gently brush the colt's graceful legs.

She began humming softly, and Star turned his neck, resting his chin on her back as she smoothed the brush down to his pastern. A smile tugged at the corner of her mouth when she felt the colt wriggle his upper lip against the back of her coat. Still crouched,

Cindy reached for a hoof pick, then thought twice and dug a bottle of hoof conditioner out of the bucket instead.

"I can't pick out your feet yet, Star," she said, touching her shoulder. "Maybe by next week the doctor will give me permission to do more." She pulled the brush out of the bottle and swiped the conditioner on his coronet band and down his hoof. Star shifted his head a little, still resting it on Cindy's bent back. She felt his warm breath at the back of her neck as he snuffled her blond hair. "That's hair, you know," she said in a warning voice. "Don't try to eat it."

Star let the weight of his head settle more heavily onto Cindy's back. "Excuse me, but I have to move to do your other feet," Cindy told him, hating to disturb the contented colt. She stretched her arm, trying to reach his back hoof without bothering him. She started to laugh when she realized what she was doing. "Do you think I could make a career out of being your pillow?" she asked him, reaching behind her with her right hand to tickle his soft nose.

"What a wonderfully familiar sight."

At the sound of the strange, deep voice, Cindy jumped, and Star jerked his head up. The greasy hoof-conditioner brush went flying into the bedding, and Cindy spun around to yell at the intruder who had startled them.

10

She began to snap at the man as she reached out to calm Star. The colt's nostrils flared, and his ears pricked forward as he eyed the stranger. But when Cindy saw the visitor's face, she froze, gaping at the tall, dark-haired man standing in front of Star's stall.

"Ben al-Rihani," she said, hardly able to believe her eyes. "What in the world are you doing here?"

2

THE HANDSOME HORSE OWNER FROM THE UNITED ARAB Emirates cocked his head and raised his eyebrows. "Is that any way to greet an old friend?" he asked in perfect English, his dark eyes sparkling with amusement.

Cindy struggled to regain her composure. "You surprised me, sneaking up like that," she said defensively. She stroked Star's tense neck. "And you surprised Star," she added.

"I apologize," Ben said sincerely. "It was just that seeing you with this colt made me think of the way you used to take care of Champion at my father's estate in Dubai."

Cindy stared at Ben. "That was a long time ago," she said. "I had almost forgotten I worked for your father."

"And Champion?" Ben asked. "Had you forgotten him, too?"

"Never," Cindy said emphatically. "Champion is still the greatest Thoroughbred Whitebrook ever trained."

Ben held his hand out to Star, who snuffled at the man's palm, then blew out noisily when he realized Ben didn't have any treats for him. Star nudged Cindy as if to point out to her that she had quit grooming him.

"He reminds me a great deal of Wonder's Champion," Ben said, gazing at the alert colt.

"He should," Cindy said, plucking the sticky hoof brush out of the bedding. "Wonder's Star and Wonder's Champion have the same dam." She started to pick the bits of straw from the brush, suddenly aware that she was dressed in grubby barn clothes while Ben looked like a model from a men's fashion magazine.

Ben looked at Star with renewed interest. "But not the same sire," he said, opening the stall door for Cindy.

"No," Cindy said, wrapping the dirty brush in a rag to clean later. She picked up the grooming bucket and stepped into the aisle. "Champion was the only Townsend Victory foal we had at Whitebrook. Jazzman is Star's sire."

"Jazzman?" Ben gave her a quizzical look. "I'm not familiar with this stallion."

"Jazzman belongs to Mike and Ashleigh," Cindy explained.

13

"I'd like to see him," Ben said, leaning over the stall wall to look at Star's legs. "He obviously passes some excellent traits on to his offspring."

Cindy was amused by Ben's strong interest in Star. "Mike and Ashleigh haven't sold too many outside breedings to Jazzman," she said. "They've tried to limit the number of his colts that are on the track."

"That is a very wise move," Ben said, nodding. "My father chose to do the same with Champion to keep his foals from becoming common." He tilted his head toward Star. "Does this Jazzman have a pedigree similar to Townsend Victory?"

"Not at all," Cindy said. "But if you're here to discuss breeding, you need to talk to Ashleigh and Mike." She wished she could check her hair for stray bits of straw and wipe any dirt smudges from her face. But more than anything, she wished Ben had called instead of just showing up.

"Actually, that was not why I came," Ben said. He hesitated, frowning. "But I seem to have caught you at a bad time. I'll get the things I wanted to drop off for you and I'll go."

As he started to turn away, Cindy realized she didn't want Ben to go. "How is Champion?" she asked quickly. Her mind flooded with memories of the big chestnut Thoroughbred that she had been so sorry to leave behind in Dubai.

14

Ben turned back, smiling. "He is still the crown prince of the al-Rihani stables," he said. "He is living a wonderful life in Dubai. My father dotes on that horse."

"I'm glad," Cindy said, feeling a little wistful. She was surprised to realize that after all these years she still missed Champion. "Is he still full of himself?" she asked. The stallion had always been willful, and behaved best when he was racing and had something to focus his attention on: winning.

Ben laughed. "Even at eighteen, Champion still thinks of himself as a fiery young stallion," he said. "I know that is what my father loves about him."

"It's good to hear that he's doing so well," Cindy said. "But I'm curious. If you're not here about the horses, then what brings you to Whitebrook?" She leaned against Star's stall, giving Ben a quizzical look.

"To see you, of course," Ben said, a smile pulling at the corners of his mouth. "I have some things you left behind when you left Dubai. I thought you might want them." Then his face turned serious. "I watched that last race you rode at Belmont in the fall," he said. "You appeared to be in a lot of pain. Are you all right?"

Cindy grimaced. She had been comfortable when horses were the subject of the conversation. She really didn't want to talk about her bad shoulder. "I had some surgery," she said. "I'll be ready to start racing again in no time." She smiled brightly and changed the subject. "How's your trainer?" she asked, feeling a twinge of something she couldn't quite identify. "Connie Richmond, right? She seemed very nice." Cindy had met the petite brunette the previous autumn in New York, and she had felt the same strange twinges then. *Is it jealousy?* Cindy wondered. She quickly dismissed the idea. *No way, not after all these years. I'm not a naive eighteen-year-old anymore.*

"Connie is fine," Ben said, looking pleased. "She has turned the al-Rihani stables into a first-class facility. Her training techniques have helped us build a solid reputation for breeding winners."

Cindy raised her eyebrows. "I'm surprised your father would allow a woman to run the stables. As I recall, he didn't even approve of a woman working there as a groom." She could barely keep the bitterness from her voice, surprised that after all this time she could still feel so hurt.

Ben winced. "My father is retired," he said. "He turned responsibility for the racehorses over to me a few years ago."

"Then you should bring Champion back to the United States so his foals can race in the Championship series," Cindy said. "He's been away from Kentucky for too long." The more she thought about Champion, the more she missed the stallion.

Star shoved his nose at Cindy, demanding attention. She turned to rub the little white star on his forehead, thinking of how Champion had been at the same
age, a magnificent racehorse with the fire to run and
the determination to win.

"I've thought about it," Ben replied, eyeing Star.
"I'd like to give Townsend Acres and Whitebrook
something to worry about. Breeding Champion to
United States mares would certainly open up a world
of opportunities." He ran his hand along Star's neck.
"Is this colt for sale?"

"Not a chance," Cindy said quickly. "The al-Rihanis
got Champion. I don't think Ashleigh and Mike would
give up Star, even if Christina would agree to it."

"I expected that," Ben said. "But it never hurts to
ask."

"So you're here to visit me and to try to buy
another Whitebrook stallion?" Cindy asked. She knew
her tone was sarcastic, but she couldn't help herself.
The way Ben looked at Star reminded her too much of
the way his father had admired Champion. And Sheik
Habib al-Rihani had ended up buying her precious
horse. Cindy didn't want the same thing to happen to
Christina's beloved Star.

"No," Ben said. "I really did come to see you. Ever
since I saw you in New York last fall, I've wanted to
talk to you." Ben pointed at her left shoulder. "I read

17

an article in the *Daily Racing Form* about you taking an extended leave. And I talked to a trainer at Belmont who said you'd come home to rest."

Cindy shrugged. Her rest was lasting far longer than she had imagined it would. "So you came down to Kentucky to ask about my shoulder? You could have just called, Ben. It's been twelve years since we've spoken."

"Ben!"

Cindy looked down the aisle to see Ashleigh Griffen hurrying toward them. She noticed that Ben seemed relieved by the interruption.

Whitebrook's owner had on a heavy canvas jacket over a pair of jeans and a sweatshirt. She wore no makeup, and her dark hair was tied back in a loose ponytail. Even in her forties, Ashleigh looked young and energetic.

"What a wonderful surprise," Ashleigh said, smiling brightly at Ben. She started to reach out to him, but then stepped back, glancing down at her clothes. "I'm working in the broodmare barn and I'm not dressed for greeting visitors. But when I saw the limousine out front I had to find out who was here."

"I had some business to attend to in Lexington," Ben said, gesturing at his suit and topcoat. "I tried to call, but all I got was an answering machine, so I decided to drop by unannounced." He enveloped

18

Ashleigh's small hand in both of his. "It is a pleasure to see you, Ashleigh."

"We've been so busy with foaling," she said. "I'm not surprised no one answered the phone. But I'm glad you came."

Cindy wished she felt as comfortable with Ben as Ashleigh clearly did, but instead she stood stiffly by, not even relaxed enough to offer him her hand. But Ashleigh hadn't been hurt by Ben the way she had.

"I'll leave you two alone," Ashleigh said. "I need to get back to the broodmares. If you have time, get Cindy to give you a tour of our place. I know it isn't nearly as grand as your stables in Dubai, but we're quite proud of what we've done with Whitebrook."

"You have much to be proud of," Ben replied, looking at Star again. "Do you have any stock for sale at the moment?"

Ashleigh glanced at Star, then back at Ben. "Not in this barn," she said firmly. "But we'll have several yearlings at the Keeneland auction next September. You might check back then."

Ben lifted his eyebrows. "I just might do that. We've done well with the American-bred horses we've brought over to Dubai."

Ashleigh nodded. "I read the feature article about your colt Rush Street in *Backstretch*. His performances are quite impressive."

Ben looked smug. "The al-Rihani stables intend to have the first Arabian-trained Triple Crown winner," he said.

"You're going to have some competition," Ashleigh warned him, grinning. She pointed at Star. "This fellow is getting back in condition to run in some of the Championship series races. Don't get too confident, Ben."

Ben turned to look at Star again. "I won't," he said. "But good competition is what keeps the races exciting."

"I do need to get back to the broodmares," Ashleigh said. "It was good to see you again."

When Ashleigh left the barn, Cindy turned to Star, trying not to let Ben see how tense it made her to be alone with him. "What time is your flight back to New York?" she asked.

Ben glanced at his wristwatch. "Whenever I tell the pilot I'm ready to go," he said.

"Oh." Cindy bit at her lower lip. She'd forgotten that the al-Rihanis had their own jet. "Did you want to see the rest of Whitebrook?" she asked.

"Yes," Ben said. "And I'd like to see this Jazzman who sired Wonder's Star."

"Let's go," Cindy said, gesturing for Ben to follow her out of the barn. She stuffed her hands into her coat pockets as they strolled past the paddocks where the yearlings were. They paused at the rail while Ben watched the young horses for a few minutes. He nodded in approval. "I will certainly be at the Keeneland auction next fall," he said. "I already see several foals I'd like to take home."

They walked by one pasture in which a graceful black filly stood beside a big black gelding, watching them pass. Ben paused near the fence, staring hard at the leggy two-year-old.

"That's Image," Cindy said, pausing beside Ben. "Ashleigh's brother-in-law bought an interest in her from Fredericka Graber, who owns Tall Oaks Farm."

"And who is the filly's companion?" Ben asked, leaning his forearms on the top rail.

"Pirate Treasure," Cindy replied. "He's blind now, but he makes a good baby-sitter for Image. Her registered name is Perfect Image, but her behavior is nowhere near perfect. Pirate helps keep her in line."

"How is her track record?" Ben asked.

"You would have to talk to Ashleigh's niece, Melanie, about that," Cindy said. "She's been training the filly since last fall, and they're really starting to work well together. I think Image may be another Derby contender."

Ben stared hard at the filly, who busied herself nibbling at Treasure's shoulder. "Another horse to keep an eye on," he said, following Cindy past the broodmare barn to where the Whitebrook stallions were kept.

"That's Terminator," she said. The gray stallion pinned his ears and stared at them, and Cindy turned away from the irritable horse, leading Ben past Wonder's Pride, Saturday Affair, and the unoccupied stalls of the stallions who had been turned out for the day.

When they stopped in front of a black horse, the stallion raised his nose and snorted, then shoved his head toward them. "This is Jazzman," she said.

George Ballard stepped out of his office, staring at the visitors to his barn. Cindy waved at the stallion manager, who nodded when he recognized her, and then went back to his paperwork.

Cindy reached up to rub Jazzman's throat. The horse angled his head and stretched forward, groaning softly as she scratched at the soft spot under his jaw.

"He's a magnificent animal," Ben said as they headed out of the barn.

"He's actually a show jumper by training, but Jazzman has sired some great racehorses for White-brook," Cindy said as they crossed the stable yard to where Ben's limousine was waiting.

Ben glanced at his watch again. "I should be heading back to the airport," he said. "Let me get the things I brought for you."

Ben reached into the backseat of the long black car and pulled out a paper bag.

22

Cindy frowned. "What is it?" she asked, taking the bag.

"Just a few things you forgot when you left Dubai," he said.

"You really came all the way here just to give me some old things I left behind in Dubai?" Cindy asked incredulously.

"And because I wanted to make sure you were all right," he said.

"I'm fine now," Cindy said. "Thanks to the surgery, I'll be perfect." She ignored the twinge in her shoulder that kept reminding her she was anything but fine. She glanced at the bag, curious to find out what she had left behind that Ben thought was so important he had come to Kentucky to deliver the bag himself.

"Apparently you were in such a hurry to leave Dubai that you didn't get everything packed," he said mildly.

Cindy felt heat climb in her face, and she knew she was turning bright red. "I had to leave," she said, feeling the sting of betrayal as deeply as though it had happened just yesterday. "I knew Champion was fine, and I had to get on with my own life."

Ben sighed. "I know. I just wish I understood why you had to run off the way you did, without hearing my side of the story."

Cindy shook her head in disbelief. "I heard

enough," she said. "You know why I left."

Ben frowned. "Because you weren't allowed to race my father's horses," he said.

"Yes," Cindy said curtly. "Because I'm a woman, and a woman has no business on a racehorse. Isn't that what you told your father?"

It was Ben's turn to blush bright red. "Yes," he admitted. "I suppose you did hear that much of my conversation with my father."

"I didn't need to hear anymore," Cindy said. "I had to come back to the United States, where I'd have a chance to prove just how good a jockey I am."

"And you did exactly that," Ben replied.

"Yes, I did," Cindy said defiantly. "I had to work hard, but at least I was given a chance."

"I understand," Ben said. "I've been watching your career. You've done much to be proud of."

"Thank you," Cindy said stiffly, gripping the bag with both hands.

"I really must go," Ben said. "I hope it won't be another twelve years before I see you again."

"I'm sure I'll see you at the track," Cindy replied.

Ben started to climb into the car, then paused, gazing back at Cindy. "You look wonderful, Cindy. Just wonderful," he said, his brown eyes shining. A tiny smile flickered across his face, and then he slid into the seat and pulled the door closed.

Cindy watched the vehicle start down the driveway, but she turned back to the barn before the car had left the farm. She didn't want Ben to think she was standing there watching him leave, mooning after him like some teenage girl with a crush. He didn't need to know how much his visit had meant to her.

Star watched from his stall as she walked down the aisle. "He's gone, Star. It's just you and me again, boy." She sank down onto a chair in front of the colt's stall and opened the bag.

The first thing she pulled from the bag was a framed photograph of her with Champion, taken in front of the stables in Dubai owned by Sheik Habib al-Rihani, Ben's father. The Cindy who grinned back at the camera looked so young and so confident. Cindy smiled to herself, thinking of the great dreams she had had then.

Under the photo was a neatly folded *gutrah*, the white headgear worn by Arab men to keep the sun off their heads. Cindy crushed the fabric in her hand, remembering the day Ben had given it to her. She held it to her face and inhaled, imagining she could smell the sweet, hot wind that swept across the vast Arabian desert.

Finally she reached into the bag and closed her hand around a thin book. What book would Ben think she could possibly want after all these years? But when she pulled it from the bag, Cindy knew why Ben had thought this book would be important to her. It was the diary her sister, Samantha, had given her for her eighteenth birthday.

Cindy returned the *gutrah* and the picture of Champion to the bag and set it aside. She leaned back on her chair and gazed at the cover of the diary for a moment, tracing the silhouette of the rearing horse that graced the book's flocked cover. She exhaled, then slowly opened to the first page and began to read.

3

HAPPY EIGHTEENTH BIRTHDAY TO ME! DAD AND BETH COOKED a special dinner, and we had a little party with Sam and Tor, and Mike and Ashleigh. Christina and Kevin were running around the living room pretending they were galloping on horses. It's hard to believe they are almost four and that Ashleigh is going to have another baby. It makes me feel kind of old. But hey! Eighteen is pretty old.

Sammy and Tor gave me this cool blank book to use as a diary. I got a new racing saddle from Dad and Beth, and Kevin drew me a picture of a horse eating birthday cake. Mike and Ashleigh asked if I wanted to ride Honor Bright in the Gazelle next week. I think that is the best present of all. Ashleigh and I are leaving the day after tomorrow for Belmont.

"Thanks for driving to New York with me," Ashleigh said. "I know it would have been easier to take a plane, but the doctor doesn't want me flying again until after the baby is born."

"I don't mind at all," Cindy said, keeping her attention on the traffic. She changed lanes, moving around a semi hauling a load of new cars. She exited onto the Long Island Expressway, then darted a glance at Ashleigh. "You hardly even look pregnant yet."

Ashleigh rolled her eyes. "Just wait another month or so. I'm sure I'll be as big as a broodmare."

"Do you want us to fix up a stall for you?" Cindy teased, passing a sign that directed them to the track. "We'll put you next to Wonder."

"I'd feel right at home," Ashleigh said. "I've been Wonder's midwife plenty of times."

"I'm sure she'd be glad to be there for you," Cindy said.

"Are you excited about racing in the Gazelle?" Ashleigh asked as Cindy pulled onto Elmont Road.

"Are you kidding?" Cindy parked near the track's backside gate. "I can hardly wait! The more big races I get to ride in, the sooner I'll have trainers begging me to race their best horses." She climbed from the car. "Someday I'm going to be one of the top jockeys in the United States."

"That wouldn't surprise me at all," Ashleigh said, stretching her arms above her head. "I just hope your shoulder is able to take the stress."

"It's fine," Cindy insisted, wiggling her left shoulder to show Ashleigh how flexible it was. The previous year she had shattered her shoulder when Honor Bright had bolted, throwing Cindy on Whitebrook's practice track. It had taken her some time to recover, but Cindy had pushed herself to get back in the saddle and back on the track.

To Cindy's relief, Ashleigh didn't mention her shoulder again. When they reached the aisle where Honor's stall was located, Cindy saw two men standing in front of the filly's stall.

"I wonder who that is," Ashleigh said, frowning. The men were looking intently at the Whitebrook filly, talking in hushed voices.

When they got near the stall one of the visitors turned. His dark eyes brightened when he saw Ashleigh, and he raised his hand in greeting. "Ashleigh Griffen," the bearded man said in a slightly accented voice. "It is a pleasure to see you again."

"Sheik Habib al-Rihani," Ashleigh said, smiling warmly. "What brings you to New York?"

The sheik gestured toward Honor's stall. "My son and I are here to purchase American-bred horses to take back home to the United Arab Emirates," he said. "When I heard you had a filly running at Belmont, I wanted to take the opportunity to see the quality of animals Whitebrook is producing."

"Are you staying until Sunday? Honor will be running in the Gazelle then," Ashleigh said.

"How is that chestnut stallion who won the Dubai Cup last year?" the sheik asked. "Have you set a price on him yet?"

Cindy stiffened when the sheik mentioned Champion. When they had taken the Triple Crown–winning Thoroughbred to Dubai the year before, many people had been interested in him, but Habib al-Rihani had approached Ashleigh and Mike several times with offers to buy the horse.

"Champion isn't for sale," Ashleigh said, shaking her head firmly. "He'll be standing stud at Whitebrook starting with the next breeding season."

Sheik al-Rihani smiled and nodded. "Then I won't bother you again about him."

Cindy finally looked past Sheik al-Rihani to the young man standing with him.

"I believe you have met my son, Ben," Habib al-Rihani said to Cindy.

"I was only home for a short break from college when you were in the United Arab Emirates for the horse races," Ben said, gazing steadily at Cindy. "I didn't have much time to enjoy the festivities that surround the Dubai Cup." A smile played at his lips. "Or to enjoy the visitors who came to Dubai."

Cindy found herself unable to look away from Ben.

She had thought he was cute when she met him in Dubai. Now she was sure that Ben al-Rihani, with his refined features and friendly smile, was the most handsome man she had ever seen.

He extended his hand to her, and she shook it firmly. "I understand this Champion that fascinates my father so much can be quite a difficult animal," Ben said, gazing down at her.

"Champion?" Cindy said, shaking her head. "He just needs a lot of attention."

"Cindy does an excellent job with him," Ashleigh added.

"It is amazing that such a small person can keep control of such a powerful creature," Ben said. "You must be a very talented jockey."

Cindy blushed giddily and struggled for a reply. "I love to race," she finally blurted out, cringing at how silly her words sounded.

"We will see you again before you leave New York," Sheik al-Rihani said, nodding politely to Ashleigh.

"I'm looking forward to watching you race," Ben said to Cindy.

"I'll be the one in the front," Cindy said, immediately regretting her words. She sounded more boastful than confident.

The al-Rihanis left, and Cindy turned her attention

to Honor, trying to shake thoughts of Ben from her mind. The filly's coat shone, and her eyes were bright. "Honor looks great," Cindy said to Ashleigh.

"Vic is taking good care of her," Ashleigh agreed, referring to the filly's groom. "Tomorrow morning you can breeze her on the track, then we'll lay her off until Sunday." Ashleigh pressed her hand into her lower back. "We need to find Vic so I can get to the motel room," she said. "I can't believe riding in a car tired me out, but I'm ready for a nap." They found the groom in the track kitchen, and after reviewing Honor's schedule for the next two days, Cindy drove Ashleigh to the motel.

The day of the Gazelle dawned clear and cool. Cindy and Ashleigh were at Honor's stall as the sun was starting to brighten the horizon.

"Mike called and told me to be sure you didn't overdo it," Vic told Ashleigh, rising from his chair in front of the filly's stall.

"I won't," she said, rolling her eyes. "You can go get some breakfast while Cindy grooms Honor."

When Vic was out of sight, Ashleigh picked up a currycomb and began currying Honor's glistening brown shoulder.

"Are you sure you should be doing that?" Cindy asked, bending down to pick up one of Honor's hooves.

"I'm pregnant, not suddenly made of glass," Ashleigh replied. "You sound like Mike."

"Mike is just excited about the baby," Cindy said, moving to a back hoof. "He wants to make sure you take care of yourself."

"I know," Ashleigh said. "And he wants a boy so he won't be so outnumbered," she added with a chuckle.

Honor Bright stamped the ground, drawing their attention back to her. "She's going to be magnificent today," Ashleigh said fondly, smoothing the filly's dark mane.

"She's going to be a streak of lightning, aren't you, girl?" Cindy patted Honor's muscular neck.

"Remember, the race is a mile and a furlong," Ashleigh said. "Don't let her run herself out in the first half. She needs to save some for the end. There are a couple of horses on the program who are strong closers."

Vic returned as they finished with Honor's brushing. "I'll get her set up for your race," he told Cindy.

Ashleigh decided to walk through the stables and visit with some trainers and owners she knew, while Cindy went to the jockeys' lounge to weigh in and check her equipment.

As the time for her race drew near, she dressed in Whitebrook's blue-and-white silks. She tucked the lightweight shirt neatly into her nylon riding pants and pulled on her riding boots.

When a voice came over the speakers calling the riders in the seventh race, Cindy joined the other jockeys walking through the tunnel that led to Belmont's saddling paddock. She met Ashleigh in the middle of the paddock.

"Vic wouldn't let me help saddle Honor," Ashleigh said, shaking her head.

Cindy laughed as she buckled her helmet into place. "As soon as the baby is born you'll be right back in the middle of things."

When Honor pranced by, Vic slowed her, holding the filly still. Before Ashleigh could give Cindy a leg up, a track employee stepped in, hoisting Cindy onto the tiny racing saddle.

Ashleigh gave a resigned sigh. "I guess I'm outnumbered," she said good-naturedly. She patted Cindy's knee. "Good luck out there."

"We'll be fine," Cindy replied, tucking her toes into her stirrups as Vic led them to the waiting pony horse.

When they reached the starting gate, Honor balked at first, refusing to enter the confined space. "Come on, girl," Cindy pleaded, keeping the filly's nose pointed at the chute. Finally two members of the gate crew got behind her, locking their arms around Honor's rump to propel her into the gate. Cindy heaved a sigh of relief when the door snapped shut behind them.

"So far so good," she murmured, adjusting her

position on the saddle. She felt her own heart speed up as the last horse was loaded, and she leaned forward over Honor's withers, tangling her fingers in the filly's mane. When the starting bell rang, Cindy felt the familiar, exhilarating rush as she and Honor exploded onto the track. Horses surged out of the gate on both sides of them. Cindy shifted Honor to the inside of the track with the thundering crowd of horses, watching for an opening near the rail. Honor listened well, letting Cindy direct her position.

The bay filly ran strongly, her strides powerful and sure. "You're doing great," Cindy murmured, guiding the filly into a hole between two other horses.

"It's Cunning Moves in the lead, with Streak-o'-Fire in second, Bay Rumba in third, Honor Bright running fourth, and Blazing Light in fifth."

"We have plenty of time," Cindy said over the pounding of hooves and the rhythmic whooshing sound of the horses' breath. Honor flicked her ears back at the sound of Cindy's voice.

"We don't want to burn out," Cindy told the filly, angling her closer to the rail and easing up beside the blood bay filly, Bay Rumba. Honor fought the grip Cindy had on the reins, and Cindy felt a twinge in her shoulder. She gritted her teeth, adjusting the pressure she had on the reins, forcing herself to ignore the pain. *I'll put ice on it later,* she promised herself, focusing on what she needed to do to help Honor come in first.

As they raced into the first turn, Streak-o'-Fire seemed to lose her momentum, and the rest of the field flew past the faltering gray horse.

"Streak-o'-Fire has broken down!" the announcer's voice rang out.

Cindy held Honor at a steady pace. The relentless pounding of horses' hooves on the ground seemed to echo in her shoulder, and the strain of keeping Honor under control added to her pain. But they maintained third place as they came into the straight stretch. Cindy could feel Honor's reserved energy waiting to explode. She knew they stood a good chance of winning the Gazelle.

"Three furlongs to go!" she heard the announcer call, and she leaned forward. "Now!" she cried to the running filly. Cindy could see streaks of sweat darkening Honor's shoulders. She tightened her hold on the reins and flicked her whip past Honor's line of vision, a cue to the filly to give it her all. In response, Honor snapped her ears back and dug in, stretching out to cover huge lengths of ground with each powerful stride.

They flew past Cunning Moves, who had dropped behind Bay Rumba, and Cindy smiled to herself as she caught the look of surprise on the jockey's face. "One more, girl, just one more horse!" Cindy cried urgently.

They caught up with the lead horse, but Bay Rumba, a three-year-old with an impressive win record for longer races, seemed to be running easily.

"Come on," she called to Honor, who seemed to be giving all she had. Cindy crouched over the filly's withers, pressing her knuckles into Honor's neck as they galloped along the rail. Cindy saw Honor roll her eye at the long-legged bay filly running beside them. Then she felt Honor dig in even harder.

Honor was going to do it! They were going to win the Gazelle! But suddenly they were at the finish line, and Cindy wasn't sure if they had won by a nose or lost by one.

The crowd roared as she circled Honor around. She could see the words *photo finish* flashing on the tote board. Then the numbers came up, and the stands came alive.

"Second," Cindy said, feeling slightly disappointed. She patted Honor's sweaty neck. "But you were still great, Honor."

The filly fought Cindy, straining to run more. Cindy's sore shoulder throbbed angrily as they jogged clockwise along the outside rail.

Vic met her on the track, catching Honor's reins. Cindy hopped to the ground, feeling a stab of pain jolt through her shoulder when she landed. She grabbed her saddle, grateful that it was feather-light. Vic gave her a wink and a grin. "Great job, Cindy. You were racing against a tough field."

"Thanks," she said. "I guess we did pretty well." But she was still disappointed that she wouldn't be posing in the winner's circle. Vic led the sweat-soaked bay filly toward the backside, and Cindy looked around, waving when she saw Ashleigh at the rail.

"That was great," Ashleigh said, giving Cindy a hug. "You were just a nose-bob from first."

"Honor was excellent," Cindy agreed. "Maybe later we can go over the race and see if there was something I could have done differently to give her a better edge."

"If you want to," Ashleigh said. "But I think you did a fantastic job." When they started for the backside, Sheik al-Rihani met them at the rail.

"Your horse ran a brilliant race," he said to Ashleigh. "Perhaps a more experienced jockey could have ensured a win for you?"

Cindy blinked, startled by the sheik's words.

Ashleigh shook her head firmly. "Cindy is an outstanding rider," she said. "It was a close, well-ridden race. I don't think anyone could have done better."

The sheik glanced at Cindy and nodded as if there was no more to be said about the matter. "My son and I would be honored if you two would dine with us this evening," he said.

"I would love to, but I am exhausted," Ashleigh said.

"I understand," the sheik said politely.

"Would you have dinner with me?" Ben asked Cindy.

Cindy hesitated, looking to Ashleigh for help.

"That sounds like a lot more fun than sitting around the motel with me," Ashleigh said with a laugh.

"Then the young people shall enjoy an evening out," Habib al-Rihani said.

After making arrangements for Ben to pick Cindy up at the motel, Cindy and Ashleigh continued on to the backside.

"Are you nuts?" Cindy demanded when they were out of earshot. "I can't go out to dinner with a sheik."

"You're not," Ashleigh said, stopping outside the jockeys' lounge. "Ben is the sheik's son. Besides," she added with a tiny smile, "I saw the way you two were staring at each other. I know sparks when I see them, Cindy. I think you'll have fun with Ben."

Cindy frowned. "You're not too tired to go out," she said accusingly. "You set me up!"

"Yes, I did," Ashleigh said. "You've been working way too hard. You need to get out and have some fun."

"But Ben comes from a rich and powerful family," Cindy protested. "I'm nobody."

"That is not true," Ashleigh said sharply. "You're

smart, you're talented, and you're going to be one of the top jockeys on the East Coast within a few years."

"Thanks for the vote of confidence, Ashleigh," Cindy said.

Ashleigh folded her arms across her chest and frowned at Cindy. "You'll go out with Ben tonight, and you'll have a great time, right?"

Cindy nodded. "If you say so, boss."

Beth had insisted that Cindy take a dress when she packed for the trip to New York. That evening when Cindy climbed into the back of the al-Rihanis' limousine, she was wearing the short black dress and a gold necklace she had borrowed from Ashleigh. She gazed around the spacious interior of the car, trying to act as though she rode in limousines all the time.

"If you don't mind, I'd like to eat at someplace not so . . . stuffy," Ben said. He was wearing a pair of beige slacks and a short-sleeved polo shirt—probably the most casual clothes he owned. "My father prefers more formal dining, but I would like to go somewhere less formal."

"That sounds good to me," Cindy said, relaxing a little. Maybe Ashleigh was right. She could have fun with Ben.

The seafood restaurant Ben chose was much nicer than the places Cindy usually ate at, but it was casual enough that most of the diners weren't wearing suits or elaborate dresses. Cindy thought she and Ben fit in quite nicely.

"Do you do anything besides race Thorough-breds?" Ben asked after the waiter had taken their orders.

Cindy laughed. "I groom them, exercise them, feed them, take care of them when they get sick, and clean their stalls," she said. "What else is there?"

"Do you go to school?" Ben asked.

Cindy shook her head. "I'm doing what I love," she said. "I don't have time for college right now."

The waiter brought their salads, and as they talked Cindy found herself enjoying the evening. She answered Ben's questions about being a jockey and described how thrilling it was to race the high-strung, powerful Thoroughbreds.

"My father is still very interested in that horse you rode in Dubai," Ben commented.

"Ashleigh will never sell Champion," Cindy said, taking a bite of lobster. "He's going to be a great addition to Whitebrook's breeding program."

"That's what my father says, too," Ben replied. He sighed. "I wish I knew more about the horses, but I haven't had much time to study Thoroughbreds and racing. My father bought his first racehorse a couple of years ago, and now he has three barns and two Thor-oughbred stallions."

"Do you ride at all?" Cindy asked, struggling to imagine life without being able to gallop on the track.

"Whenever I can," Ben said. "We have always had several fine Arabian saddle horses at home."

After they had finished with dessert, Ben glanced at his watch. "It is still early," he said. "Would you like to go dancing? We could go to a club."

"That sounds like fun," Cindy said.

Ben directed the limousine driver to drop them off at a popular nightclub. When they walked inside, the driving beat of drums and loud bass filled the large, crowded room. Cindy had forgotten how much she loved to dance, and for most of the night they were on their feet, dancing with abandon. The evening flew by, and Cindy was sorry when Ben suggested they call it a night.

"I had a great time," she said when Ben walked her to the door of her motel room.

"So did I," Ben said, gazing into her eyes. "Thank you for spending the evening with me." With that, he leaned down to kiss her lightly, then returned to the car.

Cindy slipped into her room, her head reeling. Ben wasn't like anyone she'd ever met. She tried to fall asleep, but her thoughts kept jumping from the excitement of the race she and Honor had run to the fun of the evening she had spent with Ben al-Rihani.

She got up and dug her new diary from her suitcase.

What a day! Ashleigh was very happy with how well Honor did in the Gazelle, and I went out with the cutest guy in the world. Ben is so polite, attentive, and sweet. I feel like Cinderella must have when she met Prince Charming. It's too bad Ben will be going back to Dubai to take care of his family's business, and I'll be going back to Kentucky tomorrow. I wonder if I'll ever see him again.

IT'S BEEN OVER A MONTH SINCE I WENT DANCING WITH BEN in New York. He's gone home and I'm back in Kentucky, but I haven't stopped thinking about him. Ashleigh and Mike have hired me as a full-time Whitebrook employee. Dad decided to send Honor to Miami for the last two months of the season at Calder Race Course, and I'm going with her. I won't be coming back to Kentucky until Christmas.

"Ian and I have decided to send Beautiful Music down to Florida with you," Ashleigh told Cindy. They sat on bales of straw near the barn door, catching some October sunlight while they cleaned tack.

"That's a great idea," Cindy said, dragging a soft rag down the cheek strap of a bridle. "Now I'll have two horses to work with."

"And I'm sure you'll be able to pick up some rides

from other trainers," Ashleigh said. "I know you'll be busy."

"Good," Cindy said. Ever since she and Ashleigh had returned from Belmont, she couldn't get her mind off Ben al-Rihani, except when she was riding. Spending several weeks in Florida would be a good thing.

She had been working out regularly, and her shoulder seemed much stronger now, bothering her less and less every day. She was sure she would do well in Florida.

Cindy leaped to her feet as a loud whinny split the air and hoofbeats drummed on the barn floor.

"Hey! Knock that off!" she heard Vic exclaim. The clatter of prancing hooves echoed in the barn, and Cindy looked through the doorway to see what was going on. Vic was attempting to bring Champion through the empty barn. Although he had a tight hold on the big chestnut horse's lead, it looked as though the stallion was the one in control, dancing and fighting his handler with every step.

"Why did you bring him here?" Ashleigh asked, following Cindy into the barn.

"He won't settle down in the stallion barn," Vic said. "Mike suggested putting him in one of these empty stalls for a couple of days to see if that would help calm him."

Cindy shook her head, watching Champion fight

Vic. "He's bored," she said, taking a few steps toward the horse. "All he wants to do is race. He hates being retired, Ashleigh."

Ashleigh nodded. "Why don't you give Vic a hand," she suggested. "Champion is just going to have to learn to settle down. He's almost six years old, and he's run all the races there are to run."

"Whoa there!" Vic said in a firm voice, but Champion reared, striking at the air with his powerful legs.

Cindy hurried down the aisle to give the groom a hand getting the agitated stallion settled.

"Champion!" she called. "Stop!"

Champion responded with a loud bang that echoed through the barn as he struck a wall with one of his hooves. The colt snorted loudly as Cindy approached.

"I'll take him," she told Vic.

"Are you sure?" he asked doubtfully. "He's ready to explode again."

But Cindy took the lead and held out her hand to Champion, who whooshed out a loud breath into her palm and struck at the ground impatiently.

"You settle down," she scolded. Champion nipped at her, and Cindy gave the corner of his mouth a quick flick with her fingers. "Don't you bite me!" she warned sharply.

Startled, the stallion pulled back, eyeing her warily.

"That's more like it," she said, frowning at him. "You miss racing, don't you, boy?"

Cindy winced as Champion struck the ground with his hoof. She hated to see the horse so unhappy. But Ashleigh was right. There were no more races for Champion to run, and at his age, to work him hard increased his chances of serious injury. He was too valuable to their breeding program to take such a risk.

"I've been ignoring you, haven't I?" she said, silently scolding herself for letting thoughts of Ben distract her from what was most important to her: the horses. "Tomorrow we'll go for a long ride," she promised the stallion. "You just need to get out for a while."

Champion swiveled his ears and eyed Cindy. She smiled, patting his neck. He stood still, letting her pet his elegant head.

"All you need is a little extra attention," she said, confident that she would be able to get the fiery horse under control. But what would happen when she left for Florida? She couldn't even think about it. She got the horse in an empty stall and checked his water.

"No one handles him quite like you," Ashleigh commented, watching from outside the stall while Cindy lavished attention on him. Champion did seem much calmer while she was with him. By the time she left the barn that evening, Champion was eating contentedly, looking much more relaxed than when Vic had brought him in.

The next morning Cindy fed the stallion and then took a long time grooming him before she worked her assigned horses on the practice track. By the time she had finished her regular chores, Champion had eaten all his hay. Cindy led the stallion out of his stall. "We'll tack you up and go for a nice long hack through the woods," she said. "I know you'll feel much better after that." But before she could get the colt in the crossties to tack him up, Champion stopped abruptly and reared, slashing at the air with his hooves.

"Stop it!" Cindy said sharply, tugging at the lead. Champion dropped his front legs to the ground, but then he snaked his head away, dancing at the end of the lead and nearly pulling Cindy's arms out of their sockets.

"If he doesn't settle down, he's going to hurt himself," Ashleigh commented from where she stood in the aisle, watching Champion tug at the end of his lead. "He acts like he's gearing up for a race. Or a fight."

"I know," Cindy said grimly. "Dad says Champion's only been getting a little handful of grain, but he still acts like a two-year-old on training rations." She circled the feisty horse. "Can't you just take it easy?" she asked him.

"Are you sure you can manage him when he's like that?" Ashleigh asked.

"Of course I can," Cindy said confidently, holding the lead as Champion wheeled around. "Once we get out on the trails, he'll calm right down. I'm sure of it."

"Okay," Ashleigh said, not sounding at all certain.

Cindy moved to the side as the agitated horse struck out with his hoof again. "Knock it off!" she yelled, gripping his lead with both hands. "Let's get you outside!" Champion flung his head up, nearly ripping the lead line away from her.

"Do you want some help?" Ashleigh asked, stepping forward.

Cindy tightened her grip on Champion's lead and shook her head. Mike would be furious if he knew Ashleigh had been handling the upset horse, risking herself and the baby. "I'll be fine," she insisted.

"Let me get you a stud chain," Ashleigh said. "You're going to need it to keep him under control until you're on his back."

"I've got him," Cindy said, taking a step forward. Champion crowded into her, shoving her off balance with his massive chest. Cindy pulled on the lead rope as she steadied herself, and Champion reared up again, pulling away from the pressure on his head. He caught Cindy's shoulder with his knee, knocking her to the side. She slammed into the wall, barely keeping

49

a hold on the lead line. Then she saw a blur of movement and the flash of silver shoes as Champion's hooves cut the air dangerously close to her head. Cindy fell backward, onto the ground, and the lead line slid from her hands.

Champion's hooves clattered on the aisle floor as he charged through the barn and out the door. Cindy heard shouts from outside as people noticed the runaway horse. She scrambled to her feet, ready to join the pursuit, braced for Ashleigh's lecture about how she should have had the stud chain on before she brought Champion out of his stall.

She turned to run after the fleeing horse, but to Cindy's horror, Ashleigh's crumpled form was sprawled in the middle of the aisle.

"Ashleigh!" Cindy screamed, dashing to her side. She dropped to her knees and swept the hair away from Ashleigh's face. Ashleigh's eyes were closed, her face pale and still. With a trembling hand, Cindy checked Ashleigh's pulse, breathing a shaky sigh of relief when she felt it. She heard someone screaming for help, and looked up to see who else was in the barn. Then she realized it was her own voice she had heard.

Dad and Beth are at the hospital with Mike. Samantha is here at Whitebrook with me, watching Christina and Kevin. No one has called to tell us what is going on. This is the worst night of my life. I keep hiding in the bathroom so the kids won't see me crying. It should have been me Champion ran over, not Ashleigh. Sammy keeps saying that this is just like when Ashleigh got knocked down by Mr. Wonderful and Christina was born early. She says everything turned out fine then, and it will now. But I don't believe it. It is way too soon for this baby to be born. I can't believe this is happening. I feel like I did when I found out my real mom and dad were dead. I want it to be a nightmare I can wake up from. But this is real. Too real.

5

IT'S LATE, AND CHRISTINA AND KEVIN ARE BOTH ASLEEP. LEN and Vic took care of all the horses tonight. I didn't want to leave the house in case someone called from the hospital. Tor came by for a while, but he had to go take care of his horses. I've chewed my fingernails down to nothing, and Sammy keeps pacing around with her arms wrapped around her. If I could just make time go backward a few hours, I would never have taken Champion out without a stud chain. This is all my fault. I hope Ashleigh's okay.

When she heard the kitchen phone ringing, Cindy slammed her diary shut and jumped to her feet. Samantha beat her to the phone, and Cindy stood beside her, gnawing at her lip, watching her sister's face.

"I'll tell her, Beth," Samantha said quietly. "Give Mike and Ashleigh our love. Bye." She turned to hang

52

up the phone and stood with her back to Cindy for a minute.

Cindy felt relief rush through her. Ashleigh was okay! But when Samantha turned to face her, tears were spilling down her cheeks.

"What?" Cindy demanded. "What is it?"

"Oh, Cindy," Samantha sobbed. "Ashleigh lost the baby."

Cindy felt the room start to spin around her, and she caught the back of a chair to steady herself. "No," she said. It couldn't be true.

"There's more," Samantha said, sinking onto one of the chairs at the kitchen table. "Ashleigh will never be able to have another baby."

"No," Cindy whispered again, nearly choking on the lump in her throat. Her hands began to tremble, and she blinked rapidly to keep the tears back. "This is all my fault."

Samantha swiped at the tears on her cheeks and shook her head violently. She caught Cindy's hand and squeezed it hard. "No one is to blame. It was an accident, Cindy."

When Cindy finished cleaning stalls the next morning, she left the barn quietly, stopping at the storage room to put the pitchfork away. Everyone had reassured her that she wasn't to blame for the accident, but she knew differently. She heard Mike's voice coming from Ian's office, and she hesitated before walking past the doorway. She wouldn't blame him if he fired her.

"I want that horse gone," Mike said in a flat voice. "I don't think I can stand to look at him again. I don't care where he goes, just get him out of here."

Cindy sagged against the wall, hardly able to breathe. How could Mike blame Champion? Her nightmare seemed to be getting worse by the hour. She pressed her hand to her mouth.

"I understand," Ian said. "I'll take care of it."

"Thanks, Ian," Mike said. He strode out of the office and walked past Cindy without seeming to notice she was there.

Cindy squeezed her eyes shut. Not Champion. She wanted to run after Mike, but she knew it wouldn't do any good.

Tomorrow, she told herself, *I'll talk to Ashleigh. Ashleigh won't let Mike sell Champion. He's too valuable. It doesn't make any sense at all.*

Cindy hurried down the barn aisle to where Champion had been confined in his stall. When Cindy walked up to him, the stallion pricked his ears and nickered at her. When she held her hand up, he nuzzled her palm. He looked so calm and gentle, Cindy wanted to cry.

"You don't even know what you've done, do you?"

she asked, running her hand down his nose. "They're going to sell you, Champion. I'll never see you again."

Champion shoved his nose at Cindy and pawed at the ground restlessly.

Cindy sighed. "You just need full-time attention, don't you?" she said. "I know what I can do. I won't go to Florida. I'll stay here and take care of you. If I spend more time with you, there won't be any more problems. They just can't send you away. I won't let them."

Champion huffed loudly and kicked out at the back wall of his stall. "I'll talk to Ashleigh as soon as I can," she promised the horse. "We have to get this straightened out before it's too late for you."

The next day Cindy borrowed Beth's car and drove to the hospital. She slipped into Ashleigh's room, a bouquet of bright flowers in her hands, her heart filled with hope that everything would be all right. But when she saw Ashleigh's still form on the bed, she froze. *I never should have come*, she realized. *Ashleigh won't want to see me.*

But as she turned to leave, her shoe squeaked on the polished floor. Ashleigh turned before Cindy could flee the room. "Don't leave," she said, gesturing for Cindy to approach the bed.

Ashleigh looked terrible. Her skin was chalky, and the dark shadows under her eyes looked like bruises.

Cindy could see the sadness in Ashleigh's face, and it tore at her heart. She set the flowers down on the nightstand and reached out to grasp Ashleigh's hand.

"I'm so sorry," Cindy said, trying not to burst into tears. "Can you ever forgive me?"

"It wasn't your fault," Ashleigh said. "I'm as much to blame as you, Cindy."

"Did you know Mike told Dad to sell Champion?" Cindy asked.

Ashleigh nodded. "We talked about it," she said softly.

"Do you really want Champion sold?" Cindy asked, her hope fading rapidly.

Ashleigh pressed her lips together, and Cindy fell silent, wishing again that she hadn't come. Everything she said was wrong.

Ashleigh looked away. "I know you love Champion," she said, gazing out the window as she spoke. "But I agree with Mike." She sighed, clenching and unclenching a handful of blanket. "I think Champion should go."

"What about the breeding program we planned for . . ." Cindy's voice faded. *How stupid can you be?* she berated herself. Ashleigh and Mike didn't care about how much money Champion could make standing at stud. No amount of money and prestige could replace what they had lost.

Cindy's words of protest died in her throat, and a dizzying, falling sensation overwhelmed her. There was nothing she could do to help Champion.

"If the Townsends don't want him, I'm sure your dad will find a good home for him." Ashleigh sank back against the pillow. "I'm really tired now, Cindy. I need to get some rest."

Cindy nodded and left the room. She hurried out of the hospital. Once she was safely back in Beth's car, she pressed her hands to her face and cried helplessly. It was several minutes before she regained enough control to drive home. She went directly to her room and shut the door, unable to face anyone. Then she picked up her diary and began to write.

Champion will be gone before Ashleigh gets home from the hospital. Mike wants it that way, and I know Dad will make it happen. I don't blame them. I know what happened is terrible, and I feel like I'm betraying Ashleigh by standing up for Champion. Ashleigh has done so much to help me. She let me stay at Whitebrook when I was just a runaway orphan that no one wanted, and she trusted me enough to let me work with the horses. If it hadn't been for Ashleigh giving me a chance, I might never have gotten my jockey's license. I owe her so much. But Champion is a great racehorse, and he trusts me. He won the Dubai Cup for me! I feel like I'm being torn in half.

*DAD AND I JUST GOT BACK FROM TOWNSEND ACRES. SINCE
they own half of Champion, Dad offered them Whitebrook's
share first. Clay Townsend wasn't interested, especially
since they just bought a new stallion to cross with their
Townsend Victory fillies. If Champion was at Townsend
Acres, I'd get to see him once in a while. I'm sort of relieved
he won't be there, though. Clay's son, Brad, is taking on
more and more responsibility for the farm, and he is such a
jerk. But now I don't know where Champion will end up.
Clay Townsend said he knows of someone looking for a stallion with Champion's bloodlines. He was making some
phone calls when we left. I hope he goes to a good home.*

Cindy closed her diary. She was sitting on her bed,
her back against the wall and her legs crossed. A cloud
blotted out the sunlight that had been filtering through

her window, darkening her room to fit her mood. She sighed and gazed out at Champion standing in his paddock. The chestnut stallion looked regal and alert. His head was up, and his ears were pricked as he gazed into the distance. Cindy felt her heart speed up at the sight. Champion had to be the most magnificent horse she had ever seen.

Suddenly Champion snorted. He struck the ground with his hoof, then wheeled and pranced along the fence line, his neck arched and his tail held high. He tossed his head, snaking his neck, then pausing to release a long, loud whinny.

Cindy sighed. Champion was so difficult, it was easy to lose patience with him. Even Whitebrook's skilled staff could barely handle the horse. Cindy handled him the best, and look what had happened when she was trying to do a simple thing such as lead him down the barn aisle. Would anyone else treat him with the respect and patience he needed?

Cindy heard the phone ring, and headed for the kitchen, answering it on the third ring.

"Hello?"

"Cindy? This is Clay Townsend."

"Yes, Mr. Townsend?" she said, her stomach dropping. For Clay to call them so quickly had to mean he had found a buyer for Champion.

"I have great news," Clay said.

"Do you want to talk to my dad?" Cindy asked. She didn't want to be the one to arrange Champion's sale.

"I don't have time," Clay said. "I just wanted to let you know that a business acquaintance of mine is on his way over to Whitebrook. He's looking for a stallion to improve his overseas breeding program, and he is very excited about Champion."

Cindy felt her legs go weak. She leaned against the wall. Overseas? "You mean they'll be bringing mares to the United States for breeding?" she asked weakly.

Clay chuckled. "No. Champion would have to be shipped to their breeding farm. Please let your father know so he can have the horse ready. My associate will be at Whitebrook in a few hours. I hope that's not a problem."

Cindy wanted to scream. *Not a problem? Of course it's a problem.* Sending Champion overseas meant she'd never ever see the horse again, not even to make sure he was happy in his new home!

She swallowed hard. "Of course. I'll let Dad know," she said quietly, and hung up the phone.

She found her father in the racing barn, going over papers in his office.

"Bring Champion in and get him groomed up," Ian said when she told him about Clay's phone call. "Len and Vic are busy getting things ready for your trip to Florida."

Cindy nodded silently and picked up Champion's

leather halter and the stud chain. Ever since Ashleigh's accident, she never led him anywhere without it.

Champion galloped across the paddock when Cindy walked to the gate. Eagerly he shoved his nose into his halter.

Cindy bit back a sob. "We're not going to go for a ride, boy," she said, fastening the chain over his nose. When she led him toward the barn, Champion pranced at the end of the line, acting more like an eager two-year-old than a mature horse. Cindy rattled the chain in warning and kept the skittish horse in check with a firm hand.

Champion was acting so obedient, it made Cindy feel sick to her stomach. If only she'd used the chain on the day of the accident, Champion never would have bolted, and none of this would be happening. But it was too late to undo what was done.

Even though it was awful to think that this would probably be the last time she groomed Champion, she had to make him look his absolute best. Champion deserved nothing less, even if it meant that she might never see her wonderful horse again.

When she tied him at the wash rack, Champion stood still, waiting eagerly for Cindy to run the warm water over his back. Cindy patted his shoulder. "You think this means you're going someplace to race, don't you?" she said sadly.

She massaged shampoo into his coat and combed conditioner into his long mane and tail. Then she rinsed Champion thoroughly and let him drink from the hose, watching as he sloshed the water lazily between his lips.

Cindy threw a sweat sheet on his back and then took the colt out to graze on the long grass behind the barn until he was completely dry. Finally she put him in crossties and began working him over with a soft rubber currycomb. Champion leaned into the pressure of her hand and arched his neck, clearly enjoying the attention.

Cindy wished she could enjoy grooming the stallion as much as Champion was enjoying being groomed, but the longer she worked with him, the more unhappy she grew.

She was sure he would be better behaved if she had more time to spend with him. But there was so much to do at Whitebrook. They couldn't afford to have a private groom for each horse. Not even Champion.

Cindy paused in her grooming to wrap her arms around the big horse's muscular neck. She buried her face against his warm coat and inhaled deeply. "I love you, Champion," she murmured. "I'm sorry I let you down."

As she began to polish his chestnut coat with a soft rag, Cindy heard voices at the end of the barn. She tensed her shoulders and settled her face into an expressionless mask. She wasn't going to let anyone see that she was upset about Champion. That would be petty and selfish, especially with what Ashleigh and Mike were going through. But inside, her heart was breaking.

"So we meet again," a familiar voice said, and Cindy whirled around, shocked to see her father escorting Sheik Habib al-Rihani and his son, Ben, through the barn. The sheik was wearing a dark suit and a red-and-white checked scarf, the traditional winter head covering for Arab men. Ben was also wearing a suit, but he was bare-headed, and looked even more handsome than Cindy remembered. In spite of the heartache she was feeling over Champion, his friendly smile made her feel a little better. And knowing that it was the al-Rihanis who wanted Champion made her feel a little less desolate about losing the horse.

"I regret that you are selling this magnificent horse under such sad circumstances," Sheik al-Rihani said, stopping several feet from Champion. Champion flared his nostrils and pointed his ears toward the man. The sheik looked the stallion over intently before he stepped closer to run a hand down one of Champion's legs.

Even though she knew there was nothing she could do, Cindy tensed, gritting her teeth to keep from begging him not to take her horse away. Champion wasn't hers, and he never would be.

"I have wanted this horse since I saw him run in the Dubai Cup," the sheik said, stepping back to gaze thoughtfully at Champion. "I'm just sorry that my good fortune is the result of another's misfortune."

"It will help Mike and Ashleigh to know he's going to an excellent home," Ian said.

"Then let us go take care of the paperwork," the sheik said, nodding in approval. He looked at Cindy and smiled. "You have done a superb job with him," he said. "You are an excellent groom."

"And a great jockey," Ben said quickly, frowning at his father.

"Oh, yes," the sheik said. "You do ride, don't you?" He turned to follow Ian.

Cindy gaped at Sheik al-Rihani as Ian led him away. She didn't just ride! She was a jockey, and a good one. But she kept her mouth shut, and Ian and Sheik al-Rihani disappeared into Ian's office, leaving Ben standing near Cindy. Cindy placed a possessive hand on Champion's shoulder and forced a smile for Ben.

"This is hard for you, isn't it?" Ben asked, looking from Champion to Cindy.

"Champion behaves better for me than for anyone else in the world," Cindy said. "He's always been special to me." She turned away from Ben and stroked the horse's sleek neck. "I would do anything for him," she said.

"Anything?" Ben echoed, giving her a thoughtful look.

Cindy nodded. "I'm going to miss him so much." She swallowed hard, then squared her shoulders and turned to face Ben again. "What will it be like for Champion in Dubai?" she asked.

"We don't have the Kentucky bluegrass for our horses to enjoy," Ben said. "But we do have very nice stables. We irrigate our pastures to keep them green and pleasant for the horses. My father prides himself on how well his horses are cared for."

"Who will be Champion's handler?" Cindy asked. "He can be hard to manage if he doesn't like the person who's taking care of him."

"That will be up to my father," Ben said, holding his hand out so that Champion could sniff his fingers. "This horse will have a private groom hired specifically for him. Father makes sure that every horse has a handler that is compatible with the horse."

A spark of hope sprang to life in Cindy's aching heart. "He hires people to fit the horses?"

Ben nodded. "That's the way it works at the al-Rihani stables," he said. "Especially for the horse my father hopes is going to turn his Thoroughbred breeding hobby into a serious business."

"How do I apply for the job?" Cindy asked.

"You?" Ben sounded shocked, but Cindy saw the glimmer of excitement in his eyes.

"You had the same idea, didn't you?" she asked.

Ben grinned. "You seem so sad," he said. "Not at all the girl I went dancing with in New York. It is clear that you have strong feelings for this horse, and if going to Dubai with him would make you smile again, then it is a good idea, no?"

"I'd do it in a heartbeat," Cindy said firmly.

"What about your life here?" Ben asked.

"Horses are my life," Cindy replied. "And I told you, I'd do anything for Champion."

Ben frowned thoughtfully. "Allow me to speak to my father," he said.

"I'll talk to him," Cindy said. "I can ask for my own job."

Ben shook his head. "It would be best if you let me bring the idea up to him. He is very old-fashioned about these things."

"What things?" Cindy asked, confused.

"Hiring a young woman to work in the stables is something he has never done," Ben explained. "But if he is sure it will be best for his new horse, he will be much more open to the idea."

"Fine," Cindy said reluctantly. She would have rather spoken directly to the sheik on her own behalf, but as she had told Ben, she would do anything for Champion, including let Ben beg his father for a job for her.

When Ben disappeared into Ian's office, Ian came out, a puzzled look on his face. He walked to where Cindy was unclipping Champion from the crossties.

"What's going on?" he asked. "Ben asked to talk privately with his father about an urgent matter. Did you tell him something bad about Champion so that they won't buy him?"

"I should have," Cindy said, running her hand along Champion's soft nose. "But no. I just asked if they'd hire me as his handler."

"But Cindy," Ian protested, "Champion is going to Dubai."

"I know," Cindy said calmly, feeling more sure about this decision than anything else she'd ever done. "I've been there before. I think it would be a great place to live."

"But what about the cultural differences?" her father tried to argue. "Women are treated very differently in Arab countries."

Cindy stared steadily at Ian. "I know it will be difficult," she said. "You just don't want me to go."

"Of course I don't," Ian said. "But I also don't think you realize what you're getting into."

"Champion is my responsibility," Cindy said stubbornly. "I let him down, and I let Ashleigh down, too. I won't let it happen again."

Ian frowned. "No one is blaming you for what happened, Cindy."

Cindy looked from her father to Champion. The horse gazed back at her with his keen brown eyes. "I am," she said quietly. "If the sheik will hire me, I'm going. That's all there is to it."

"We'll talk later," Ian said. He walked away, leaving Cindy to put Champion in his stall. She knew her father didn't like the idea of her going so far away. But Cindy was certain that going to Dubai with Champion was the right thing for her to do. And if Ian wanted what was best for her, he wouldn't stand in her way.

When voices sounded from Ian's office, Cindy looked in that direction. Ben and his father were walking out of the office. The sheik was frowning and shaking his head, but Ben was nodding and talking rapidly in Arabic, pointing in Cindy's direction, then gesturing at Champion. The sheik looked intently at the colt, who had hung his head over his stall door and was nuzzling Cindy's hair.

Habib al-Rihani sighed and raised his hands in a gesture of surrender. Cindy smiled, and a little tremor of excitement shimmied up her spine. Clearly Ben's father had given in. She was going to Dubai with Champion.

That evening she sat at the little desk in her bedroom, a blank pad of paper in front of her. Finally she grabbed her diary and began to write.

I need to make lists of all the things I have to get done by Christmas. I'm supposed to leave for Dubai at the beginning of the year. I'm having a hard time believing this isn't a dream. It doesn't seem real, but it is. Champion and I are going to Dubai!

7

IT SEEMED AS THOUGH IT TOOK FOREVER TO GET ALL THE PAPER-work taken care of, but I'm finally on the plane! Sheik al-Rihani had a stall built into the cargo hold especially for Champion. I hated to leave him alone down there, but the veterinarian tranquilized him before we loaded him, so he should be all right.

Living in a foreign country is going to be cool. I promised I would send lots of letters home. The only problem is that I hate writing letters. At least Sammy is excited for me. She says she's jealous, and she reminded me that I'm going to be living in the same house as Ben. As if I needed reminding! Dad tried so hard to act happy, but I know he and Beth are both worried about me. I kept telling them I'm going to be fine.

I need to find out how to get my jockey's license approved in the UAE. There are plenty of world-class races held there, and I want to ride in all of them. I'm going to come back to the United States as an internationally famous jockey.

"Please fasten your seat belts. We're preparing to land at Dubai International Airport," the flight attendant announced.

Cindy closed her diary and tucked it into her carry-on bag. She sat straight, looking over the tops of the seats to the front of the plane, where the flight attendant stood with a microphone in her hand.

Most of the heads Cindy could see had dark hair or were covered with scarves. She reached up to touch her short blond hair, wondering for the first time if she was going to fit in at all in Dubai.

"As you can see from the windows," the flight attendant continued, interrupting Cindy's thoughts, "Dubai is a large, active seaport city on the Persian Gulf. The city is divided by Dubai Creek, a ten-mile-long deepwater channel. To the east of Dubai is a vast desert known as the Rub al-Khali, or Empty Quarter, where the lost city of Ubar is hidden somewhere beneath the miles of barren sand."

Cindy peered out the plane's window at Dubai. Tall, modern skyscrapers shadowed the domed tops of old buildings. Sunlight glinted off the Persian Gulf,

71

and she could see Dubai Creek cutting through the center of the city, dotted with tiny white specks she assumed were boats.

The plane banked, and Cindy braced herself. She wished she could be with Champion to reassure him during the landing, but there was nothing she could do right now. The plane shuddered slightly as they approached the runway, and Cindy sighed with relief when she heard the screech of the tires touching the ground.

As the plane taxied to a stop, Cindy realized her hands were trembling. *With excitement, not nerves,* she told herself. She and Champion were going to have a great time living in Dubai. She rose, clutching her small carry-on bag tightly as she joined the passengers exiting the plane.

Most of the conversation that flowed around her was in Arabic, and it dawned on Cindy that she would need to learn at least a little of the language. She'd had trouble with her French class at Henry Clay High School, but French was nothing compared to Arabic. Cindy shook her head. She wasn't sure she would ever be able to decipher the words.

To her relief, the signs to the baggage claim area were in English as well as Arabic, and soon she was waiting in the line to get through customs. It seemed to take an eternity as the agents looked in suitcases, asked questions, and directed travelers to their next stop. Cindy watched with alarm as a man ahead of her was escorted away by a uniformed guard.

The customs agent took her papers and frowned as he read them over. Cindy watched him anxiously. She knew she had done everything she was supposed to, but his scowling expression made her nervous. She breathed a sigh of relief when he returned her papers and waved her through.

She stood in the middle of the terminal, feeling a little lost as travelers swept past her. She watched people greet each other with hugs and smiles. Many of the men had full beards, and their heads were covered with checked cloths like the one Sheik al-Rihani had worn. A small group of women wearing long black robes, with veils covering their faces, clustered together, watching as passengers came into the terminal. Cindy tried not to stare, but she had trouble not gaping at the different sights and sounds.

Cindy was relieved by the wide variety of people she saw in the terminal. Many of the women wore Western-style clothing, mostly suits and dresses, with their heads and faces left uncovered. But when several more veiled women walked by, Cindy reached up to touch her bare cheek. She hoped the al-Rihanis wouldn't expect her to cover her face.

"Cindy!"

She spun around when she heard her name, and was delighted to see Ben hurrying toward her. Cindy raised her hand in greeting.

"I'm glad you're here," Ben said, stopping in front of her.

"Thanks," she said, suddenly feeling shy.

Ben looked at the small bag at her feet. "Is this it?" he asked, picking up her single suitcase.

When she nodded, he tilted his head toward the doors. "Then shall we go out to the van? I'm sure you want to see Champion and get to your new home."

"Thanks, Ben," she said, glad he understood how she felt. "I know Champion can't wait to get off the plane. I hate to leave him there a moment longer than I have to."

"Do you have his import papers?" Ben asked, winding his way through the throngs of people.

Cindy dug an envelope stuffed with papers from her purse. "Right here," she said. She didn't tell him she had checked every few minutes throughout the long flight just to reassure herself that she still had all the documents.

"This way," Ben said, leading her to a horse van in the parking lot. He drove to a large gate, where he presented Champion's papers, and the guard waved them through. Ben stopped near the plane.

"Do you need help?" he asked as Cindy headed for the cargo bay.

"No, thank you," Cindy said politely. She had been working with him daily until they left the United States, and Champion had been much better behaved, but she didn't know how he was going to act when he first came off the plane.

"How are you doing, boy?" she asked, clipping a lead line to his halter. The big stallion followed her out of the stall but walked onto the ramp with cautious steps, his head high. He stopped halfway down, his nostrils flared wide as he took deep, snorting breaths of the strange air. A warm breeze swept over them, and Cindy reached up to stroke the stallion's tense neck. "It's okay, boy," she said quietly. "You've been here before. Doesn't it smell familiar?"

Champion looked around, his ears pricked sharply. Cindy gritted her teeth, ready for an explosion, and tightened her grip on the stud chain she had looped over his nose. But Champion exhaled and gave her shoulder an affectionate nudge with his nose.

Cindy smiled. "Maybe you know this is your new home," she murmured, leading him down the ramp and away from the plane. Champion pranced a little, skittish after being in the hold for so many hours.

"You'll be okay," Cindy said, patting his neck as

she walked beside him. "Let's get you into the van and to your new home."

Ben grinned at Cindy. "He is magnificent," he said. "I understand why my father wanted him so badly. And I'm so pleased that you were able to come to Dubai with him."

"Me too," Cindy said. When they reached the back of the van, Champion stopped. He snorted and struck at the ground nervously, eyeing the opening.

"It's all right," Cindy said, giving him a reassuring pat. "This won't be nearly as long a ride."

The stallion balked for a moment, looking as though he wanted to wheel away and run, but Cindy kept talking to him and stroking his neck. For a few tense minutes she wondered if they were going to end up walking to the al-Rihani estate. But finally Champion stuck his nose inside the van and sniffed the walls, floor, and ceiling. Then he heaved a sigh and walked inside. Soon Cindy was seated in the cab next to Ben, heading for the al-Rihanis' home, south of the city.

When they passed a herd of camels grazing beside the road, Cindy twisted in her seat to stare at the strange creatures. "I'm used to driving past fields full of Thoroughbreds," she commented.

Ben laughed. "It isn't quite like Kentucky, is it?"

"No," she said, gazing across a stretch of sandy

ridges, feeling a little homesick for the green pastures full of horses she had left behind.

"Just wait," Ben said. "We'll go to the camel races, and you'll see what one of the 'ships of the desert' can do on a track."

"I thought camel races were just a joke," Cindy said, laughing.

"No," Ben replied. "Camels are very important to the Arab nations. For centuries camels have provided food, clothing, and transportation for the desert people. Camel racing is as serious here as horse racing. There are even special tracks, and the competition is very fierce."

When they passed a group of people standing at the side of the road, Cindy noticed that the women were completely covered except for their eyes. She twisted in her seat to keep the group in sight. "Why do only some women cover their faces?" she asked.

"The UAE is much more open than some of the other Arab countries," Ben said. "In some places it is considered immodest for women to expose their faces, and it brings dishonor to their families. Here the women you see wearing veils belong to certain religious sects where those beliefs still hold true. But for the most part, the women in the UAE are free to wear what they please."

"So I won't be expected to cover myself from head to toe with robes and veils?"

Ben laughed. "No, but remember that some of the traditional clothing serves as protection from the sun and the sand, which is why the ancient styles have endured for centuries."

Cindy felt her jaw drop when the al-Rihanis' villa came into view. The estate filled a small, fertile valley, and the buildings were surrounded by sprawling green pastures and orchards. Cindy could see a large white stucco barn and row upon row of white-fenced paddocks. On a knoll several hundred feet away was the house, a two-story pink clay building with a flat, red tiled roof. Orchards of olive and fig trees covered part of the land, and near the barns Cindy could see the defined oval of a racetrack.

"This is going to be great," she said excitedly. "I can hardly wait to ride on the track. Do you have any horses ready to race?"

"My father is working on that," Ben said. "Our current two-year-olds are Father's first home-bred racehorses. We have a few almost ready for the track now."

Ben parked away from the main stable, near a smaller building. Cindy noticed there were no other horses in sight, but as they climbed from the rig a small, dark-haired man approached them.

"Jamal," Ben said, "this is Miss Cindy McLean. She

is the assigned handler for Wonder's Champion, my father's new stallion."

Jamal nodded politely to Cindy, then turned his attention to the horse van. "I am curious to see this new horse," he said. "The sheik has talked of nothing else for the last several weeks."

When Cindy led the chestnut horse from the van, he dropped his head to sniff the ground. "It's all right, boy," she said, watching the stallion closely.

"He is godlike," Jamal said in an awed voice.

"I'll take your things up to the house," Ben said. Before Cindy could protest that she planned to stay in the stables, he was gone, leaving her with Jamal.

Champion lifted his head and whinnied loudly, then waited for an answering call.

Jamal gestured toward the nearby stucco building. "This is where Champion will stay for now," he said. "As soon as the sheik's veterinarian gives approval, he will be moved to the stallion barn with the sheik's two other Thoroughbred stallions."

The interior of the isolation stable was sparkling clean, with whitewashed walls and a high ceiling. Cindy led Champion to his new stall, a spacious box with deep, soft straw. Jamal pointed out the small bathroom and the tack room, which held a cot and a trunk, along with the shelves and racks that held the horses' supplies and tack.

"I'll leave you to get him settled. My son, Kalim, will bring feed and fresh water," Jamal said.

"Thank you," Cindy replied. Then she was alone with Champion. The horse released another long, loud whinny.

"Your friends from Whitebrook aren't here," Cindy said. "But you'll make new friends."

Champion darted a look at her, then spun in the stall, sniffing at the walls and striking at the bedding. In a minute he wheeled around and whinnied loudly again, his entire body shaking with the effort.

"It's okay, boy," Cindy said, patting his shoulder. "You'll get used to this." She ran her hand along his shoulder and sighed. "We're both going to be just fine. We'll let you get adjusted for a couple of days, then we can go for a ride, okay?"

Finally Champion relaxed enough to drop his head and nuzzle her shoulder. Cindy rubbed his forehead, trying to soothe him with quiet words and gentle pats.

The soft slapping of sandaled feet on the cement floor drew her attention, and Cindy turned to see a teenage boy burdened with a large bucket of water and an armload of hay.

"Hi," she said, smiling at him.

He started to smile back, then he looked past her and his eyes widened. Cindy glanced over her shoulder. Champion stood in the middle of the stall, his magnificent head highlighted by a shaft of sunlight. To Cindy, the stallion had never looked more majestic. His dark chestnut coat gleamed, and the angles of his elegant head were accented by the light. She understood why the boy was staring at the horse, and she reached over to run her hand along the stallion's graceful neck.

"This is Champion," she said proudly. She pointed at the hay. "Is that for him?"

"For Champion," he said in halting English. He held the hay out, and Cindy put it in Champion's manger. The horse sniffed at the water, then turned away to inspect the hay. He took an experimental bite, then chewed thoughtfully, gazing at the boy who stood outside the stall.

"I'm Cindy," she said, pointing at herself.

"Kalim," he said, grinning as he pointed at himself.

He extended his hand to Champion, who sniffed at the boy's fingers, then bobbed his head. "I think he likes you," Cindy said, nodding in approval.

Kalim shot her a quick smile, then crooned to Champion in Arabic. Cindy had no idea what he was saying, but Champion seemed to like the sound. He leaned forward, pricking his ears, letting Kalim run his hand along his sleek jaw. Champion snuffled Kalim's dark hair, lipping it curiously, then curling his lip at the taste.

Cindy and Kalim laughed at the horse's expression. "I think you've already made a new friend, Champion," Cindy said.

When Ben returned, Kalim darted a quick smile at Cindy and slipped quietly out of the stable.

"The other facilities are much nicer, as you will soon see," Ben said. He gestured toward the door. "As soon as you get settled I'll take you on a tour."

Cindy glanced at Champion. "I don't want to leave him alone yet," she said. "He isn't ready for it."

"Kalim!" Ben called. The boy came from just outside the door, looking eager. Ben spoke to him in Arabic, and Kalim grinned broadly, his eyes settling on Champion.

As Ben spoke, Kalim nodded happily, stepping close to Champion's side.

"There," Ben said. "I saw how Champion took to Jamal's son. The boy has a way with horses. Now Champion won't be alone, and you can see where you will be living."

Cindy hesitated, but Kalim was already stroking Champion's shoulder and talking to the big horse. Champion dropped his head, looking quite calm, so Cindy followed Ben out of the stable.

"I thought I'd stay in the barn," she said. "All I need is a cot so I can be near Champion. I'm sure I'll be comfortable there." She was certain she'd be more at home with the horses than in the al-Rihanis' stately home.

"My mother would never hear of it," Ben said, shaking his head. "Most of our employees live nearby. Only a few stay at the stables."

When they went inside the house, Cindy was awed by the elegant furnishings, the beautiful paintings, and the graceful sculptures that decorated the rooms. She was careful not to touch anything, painfully aware that she had just come from the barn.

Ben gestured at an arched doorway, and Cindy peered around him. Outside she could see a courtyard filled with lush greenery. A tall, slender woman rose from a chair beneath a palm tree. Her brightly colored dress swirled around her calves as she crossed the courtyard. "You must be Cynthia," she said, extending her hand and smiling warmly at Cindy. "I am Zahra al-Rihani."

Cindy immediately liked Ben's mother. "I'm very pleased to meet you," she said sincerely.

"I am delighted to have you here," Zahra said. "My husband is very excited about this wonderful race-horse you have brought with you."

Cindy laughed. "It's more like Champion brought me here," she said.

"Would you like some tea?" Zahra asked, waving at the table under the tree. "I can have Nura bring cups."

"No, thank you," Cindy said. All she really wanted was to get back to the barn and make sure Champion was all right.

"Let me show you the rooms we prepared for you," Mrs. al-Rihani said, sounding excited about what she had done for Cindy.

"I'll meet you down at the stables when you've unpacked," Ben said. "You can visit the rest of the barns and see our other stallions."

"And the racehorses," Cindy reminded him.

"Are you packed for your trip tomorrow?" Ben's mother asked him. "Do you want me to take care of anything for you?"

"I'm all ready to go," he replied, winking at Cindy. "She thinks I'm still twelve and not twenty," he said. He gave his mother a kiss on the cheek before he left the room.

Cindy watched him go, a sinking feeling taking hold of her. *Ben is leaving tomorrow?* She wondered where he was going and how long he was going to be gone.

Zahra turned back to Cindy. "I hope you will be happy living here."

"I'm sure I will," Cindy said politely.

"I took the liberty of having your luggage placed in the maid's quarters," Zahra said, gesturing for Cindy to follow her. "Not that I consider you unworthy of rooms in the main house," she added quickly. "But the maid's rooms overlook the stables and have a private entrance, so you can come and go as you please. My intention was to allow you some privacy."

"Thank you," Cindy said, touched by Zahra al-Rihani's thoughtfulness. She didn't know how to tell the kindhearted woman that she would rather be in the stables, not after all the trouble Mrs. al-Rihani had gone to. She followed the woman, crossing the gleaming floor with careful steps, afraid her shoes might smudge the polished tiles.

When she walked into the apartment, Cindy gaped at the combination sitting room and bedroom, with its light-colored furnishings. It was so luxurious, she felt uncomfortable. She didn't belong in a room like this.

When Zahra led the way onto the small patio off the entrance, Cindy had a clear view of the stables. "This is very nice," she said, eyeing the stables longingly. She wondered how Champion was doing.

"Come to the courtyard as soon as you've unpacked," Mrs. al-Rihani said. "We can visit."

"I think I had better—" Before Cindy could finish her sentence, the sharp sound of a loud bang carried up from the stables. Cindy caught her breath, listening intently. It came again, the unmistakable sound of a horse's shod hoof kicking a stall wall. She heard shouting, then saw men running toward the isolation barn.

"Something's wrong!" she exclaimed. Cindy took off for the stables at a swift run, leaving Zahra al-Rihani standing on the patio.

When I heard all the banging in the barn, I was so worried about Champion that I forgot all about Ben's mom. I'm sure I made a horrible first impression on her. I don't think Mrs. al-Rihani understands that I would rather be in the barn than in that fancy room she fixed up for me. I came here to take care of Champion, not to sleep in a room full of antiques and silk cushions.

8

IT FELT LIKE A NIGHTMARE. I WAS RUNNING AS FAST AS I COULD, but the barn was so far from the house, I thought I'd never get there. The house is on a hill overlooking the rest of the estate, so I was running downhill, trying to keep from tripping over rocks and falling. All I could hear was Champion whinnying and kicking the walls of the stall and the men shouting from inside the barn. I was so afraid he would hurt himself.

As Cindy got closer to the barn she heard Champion whinny frantically, and her heart caught at the desperate sound. A moment of silence was followed by a series of loud cracks that she knew were his hooves striking the stall again and again.

She dashed inside to see a group of white-robed men gathered in front of Champion's stall. Cindy caught glimpses of Champion as the horse paced back and forth. To her relief, the stallion appeared to be fine. She paused by the door to catch her breath, gasping for air after her frantic run from the house.

The men were arguing loudly among themselves. Cindy didn't need to understand Arabic to know they couldn't agree on which one of them was going to go into the stall and try to get Champion under control. None of them seemed too eager to get close to the agitated horse. When one of them started toward the stall, Champion wheeled around and aimed a powerful kick at the door, connecting with an earsplitting crack. The man jumped back, and the arguing began again.

Cindy stepped forward. "Excuse me," she said, trying to get around the men.

They turned to stare at her, but none of them would move to let her get close to Champion. The oldest-looking of the group frowned at her and shook his head firmly, blocking her way to the stall.

"Let me by," she said more forcefully. "I can handle him." *And I should have been here with him,* she scolded herself. *I never should have let Ben talk me into letting Kalim watch Champion.* "He's my responsibility," she said, glaring at the bearded man, who seemed to be in charge.

He gave her a puzzled look and shook his head, saying something in Arabic. Behind the wall of men,

88

Champion pawed at his bedding, then lunged at the stall door, rolling his eyes so that the whites flashed. The men jumped back as Champion spun around to aim another kick at the already damaged stall door.

"Where is Ben?" Cindy asked desperately. There had to be someone around who spoke English. She needed to make these men understand that she was in charge of Champion.

The man shrugged and folded his arms across his chest. With a growl of frustration, Cindy shoved past him and marched into the stall.

"Champion," she said loudly, "you settle down."

Champion whipped his head around and pressed his nose into Cindy's chest, sniffing her all over and grunting softly.

From the corner of her eye, Cindy could see the men looking from her to Champion in surprise. The one who seemed to be in charge gestured for the rest of them to move back.

"I'm here," Cindy reassured the stallion, massaging his neck gently. She felt terrible for leaving him alone so soon after they had arrived. "Where is Kalim?" she asked him. "Did you scare him away?" Champion's coat was streaked with sweat, and he flashed the whites of his eyes as he looked at the men standing outside the stall.

"It's all right," Cindy said in a soothing voice,

stroking his tense shoulder. She let herself into the stall, and Champion crowded close to her. She could feel him trembling, and she gently stroked his neck, murmuring soft, calming words to him.

"What is going on here?" a forceful voice demanded from the stable door.

Cindy looked up to see a glowering Sheik al-Rihani standing in the doorway. Beside him stood Jamal, looking anxiously from Cindy to the group of men in front of Champion's stall.

The bearded man who had been speaking began gesturing at Champion and Cindy, talking rapidly. It frustrated Cindy that she couldn't tell what he was saying, but as he spoke, the sheik's face grew stern. He directed a dark look in Cindy's direction. Finally Sheik al-Rihani nodded and gestured at the door. The men filed out of the stable in silence.

"He doesn't like his new accommodations?" the sheik said in a mild voice, eyeing Champion from across the barn.

"It isn't that," Cindy said quickly. "I think he was more upset about being left alone so soon."

"I thought we agreed you would be with him at all times," the sheik said, frowning at her. "That was the arrangement when I agreed to let you accompany him to Dubai, was it not?"

Cindy caught her next words before she answered.

She wasn't going to get Ben in trouble by telling his father that he had insisted she leave Champion with Kalim. She was here to take care of Champion, not go wandering off with Ben al-Rihani.

"I'm sorry," she said quietly. "I'll be with him day and night from now on."

The sheik nodded. "You will have your days off, of course," he said. "But until Champion gets settled, you must be on duty full time."

Cindy nodded. "I understand," she said. "I want him to feel comfortable and happy here. I won't leave him."

"I'm glad we are in agreement," the sheik said. "This horse's good health is very important to my vision for the al-Rihani stables." Without another word, the sheik turned and strode out of the stable.

Jamal hesitated in the doorway. "I'm sorry," he said. "The man who handles the broodmares called for Kalim to help him with a mare in labor. My son would never have left Champion alone otherwise. He is a very responsible boy."

Cindy nodded. "It's my fault, really. I'm responsible for Champion," she said.

"My men are not accustomed to handling horses of Champion's temperament and size," Jamal added. "The Arabians we have here are very gentle, social animals, and the other two Thoroughbred stallions don't seem to have your horse's aggressive traits."

"Champion just needs to get used to everything," Cindy said quickly. "He'll settle down. But the sheik is right. I had no business leaving him."

When Jamal left, Cindy began grooming Champion, rubbing his damp coat with a soft rag. "I really messed up, boy," she said. "First day on the job and I'm already in trouble with the boss."

Champion began to relax in Cindy's familiar presence. Soon he was calm, moving just enough to let her know where he wanted to be brushed the most. She laughed when he shifted his weight off his left leg, dropping his hip so she could brush his croup. "You are the most spoiled horse in the world," she said, reaching up to run the brush along his back. Champion groaned contentedly in response.

When Ben came looking for her later, she refused to leave Champion. "He just gets too upset," she said. "The tour will have to wait."

Ben shrugged. "Fine," he said. "But tomorrow I'm leaving for France. I won't be back for a couple of weeks."

"Oh," Cindy said, barely hiding her disappointment. She resumed grooming Champion. "That sounds like fun."

"Not really," Ben said. "It's a business trip." He rested his arms on top of the stall door, watching her.

"I'll show you all of Dubai when I get back, okay?"

With that, Ben left the stable, and Cindy turned to Champion. "It looks like we're going to need each other, boy," she said. "I don't have any other friends here."

Even though it was mid-January, the weather had been hot and sunny all day. Now, as the shadows grew long, the air started to cool. Cindy looked around the stable for a blanket to wrap up in. She found a clean horse blanket in the tack room, then washed her face and hands in the tiny bathroom. She'd worry about her luggage later. Her stomach rumbled, reminding her that the last thing she had eaten was the meal they had served on the plane. "It won't kill you to miss dinner," she said out loud, trying to ignore the gnawing in her stomach. She couldn't leave the stable to find any food. She wasn't going to let Champion out of her sight until he was relaxed and completely comfortable in his new home.

She draped the blanket over her shoulders and sat on the bales of straw against the wall. The rhythmic, familiar sound of Champion munching his hay soothed her, and slowly her eyes drifted shut. It had been quite a long day.

"Cindy?"

She sat up abruptly when she heard her name, thinking for a moment it was Beth or Samantha. But it was Zahra al-Rihani who came into the stable, carry-

93

ing a tray. She was followed by a woman wearing a white apron over a dark dress, her arms loaded with blankets.

"My husband explained that you preferred to stay with the horse," Ben's mother said, glancing around the stable with a disapproving look. "Nura and I brought you some bedding and food." Zahra eyed Champion, who flared his nostrils and rolled his eye at her. "I wish I could convince you to sleep in the house."

"Champion needs me," Cindy said, shaking her head. Her stomach rumbled when she smelled the spicy aroma rising from the tray Zahra held. "Thank you so much, but I'll be very comfortable right here."

Zahra handed her the tray, and Cindy resisted tearing the cover off to see what smelled so wonderful.

"If you change your mind," Zahra said, "the outside doors to your quarters will be open."

"Thank you," Cindy said, watching Nura make a tidy bed out of the cot. She smiled at the two women. "I'm very grateful," she said sincerely.

"We will leave you to care for your horse," Zahra said, giving Champion another wary look before she left the stable, the maid at her heels.

Cindy couldn't identify the food she ate, but it was warm and spicy, and when she had cleaned the plate, she felt deliciously full and tired.

She dragged the cot against Champion's stall and settled in for the night, her mind reeling with the events of the day. Champion hung his head over the stall wall, and she could feel his warm breath on her. Cindy reached up to give the horse's nose a soft pat, then pulled her diary from her suitcase, which Nura had left beside the cot.

My first day in Dubai was definitely an experience I'll never forget. I wanted to make such a good impression on the al-Rihanis, but instead the sheik got angry with me for leaving Champion alone. Mrs. al-Rihani had such a beautiful room all ready for me, and instead I'm sleeping on a cot in the barn. I'm sure they don't know what to think of me. I was glad to find out I don't have to wear the robes and face coverings like so many of the women I saw today. Tomorrow I'll go to the racing barn and see the two-year-olds in training. I wonder which ones they'll let me ride.

9

I'VE BEEN IN DUBAI FOR ALMOST TWO WEEKS. I THINK CHAM-*pion is adjusting better than I am. He is in the stallion barn now, and I'm staying in the grooms' quarters there. Kalim spends lots of time with us, practicing his English and helping me with Champion. I wish Ben would come home. His mother stays away from the stables. I think she's afraid of horses. I've gone up to the house for tea a couple of times, but I'd rather be in the barn. It is fun to watch the handlers take the horses to their paddocks in the morning. Instead of jeans they all wear long white robes. Jamal told me the robes are called* dishdashahs. *There is a beautiful gray colt called Wyndrake that I would love to ride, but Jamal won't let me handle any of the horses except Champion. I haven't ridden at all since I got here. I'm beginning to wonder if they will ever let me ride.*

Champion pawed his bedding, eager to get out of his stall. Cindy stuffed her diary in Champion's grooming box and stood up, sweeping bits of bedding from her jeans. Daily walks and constant attention had helped the stallion adjust to his new life, but he was still energetic and eager to go. Cindy was pleased that the horse was doing so well, but she wanted to saddle him up and give him a chance to work on the track. "I know you miss it," she murmured to the stallion. "I miss it, too."

She clipped a lead onto his halter and led him from the stall. Champion danced at the end of the lead.

"Where are you going?" Jamal asked as they left the barn.

"For another walk," Cindy said. She patted the horse's arched neck. "What I'd really like to do is take him for a ride. Do you think I could tack him up?"

Jamal shook his head firmly. "The sheik's orders," he said. "He has invested a great deal in this horse, and he doesn't want to risk anything happening to him."

Cindy clamped her mouth shut. As if she wanted something bad to happen to Champion! She could handle him even better up in the saddle than from the ground. As soon as the sheik returned from his trip with Ben, she would talk to him about riding Champion.

Champion pranced down the middle of the aisle,

his neck arched and his steps high, as though showing off his magnificent conformation to the other stallions in the barn. She could see the other grooms gaping at him, and she felt her heart swell with pride. He was the finest-looking stallion on the sheik's estate, she was certain of that.

Once they were out of the barn, Cindy led Champion by the training track. Champion paused to sniff at the ground and snorted loudly.

"I know how you feel," Cindy said. "I'd like to take a gallop around the track, too."

Instead they walked past the track and along the dirt lane that wound through the al-Rihanis' olive orchard. The sun beat down on Cindy's head, as it had every day since her arrival. Cindy was careful to use sunscreen, but her skin was already tanned and her hair was a shade blonder. She could see now why the Arabs wore robes and head coverings to protect themselves from the hot sun.

When she returned Champion to his stall later, Jamal was just leaving his small office at the back of the barn.

"Champion seems to be content here," Jamal commented.

Cindy nodded. "Since he's doing so well, do you think I could start working some of the racehorses?" Cindy had been avoiding the training barn. None o the grooms there spoke English, and whenever she walked by, they all began talking in Arabic, making her wonder what they were saying about her. But if she could get on the track with the exercise riders in the morning, she could show them just how much they had in common. Maybe then they would be a little friendlier.

Jamal gave her a startled look. "But you are Champion's handler," he said.

Cindy nodded. "I'm also a professional jockey."

"You will need to speak to the sheik about riding other horses," Jamal said. "Champion is the most valuable horse in the stable and worthy of a full-time handler. If you are exercise-riding and racing, that would interfere with your job."

Cindy sighed. She knew she could take care of Champion and do some riding. But she didn't argue with Jamal. She would take it up with the sheik upon his return—when the time was right.

The day after Ben and his father returned from their trip, Ben gave Kalim orders to look after Champion and drove Cindy and his mother into Dubai. After a lunch of spicy eggplant and grilled chicken served with pita bread, Ben left his mother and Cindy at the al-Dhiyafah Road shopping center—much to Cindy's dismay.

For several hours Zahra took Cindy through fashion boutiques. Cindy smiled politely and admired dresses, jewelry, and shoes that she had no interest in. When Ben finally picked them up at the end of the day and they returned to the estate, Cindy was relieved to find Kalim singing in Arabic to Champion while the stallion dozed. It looked as though Champion hadn't even noticed she was gone.

"I knew you would both love it here," Ben said happily before he left to take care of business.

It was true, Cindy thought. Champion couldn't have been happier. But she would have been a lot happier if she had been allowed to ride. She didn't want to complain to Ben behind his father's back, though. She had been waiting anxiously for a chance to speak to the sheik about it, but he had been so busy, he hadn't been around the stables much.

Kalim was confident with the stallion, and Champion seemed exceptionally calm and attentive around the boy. In the coming weeks Cindy allowed Kalim to help her with Champion more and more, until one morning Cindy stood back and let Kalim feed and groom the horse while she wandered out to the track.

When the exercise riders came out with the two-year-olds preparing for their first races, she shook her head in disgust. She couldn't believe she was being forced to watch from the rail as the horses started their works. She could handle a horse better than any of the riders out there.

"Please let me ride," she said to Jamal, who had joined her at the rail. "I can't bear to just stand here and watch."

"I can't allow it without the sheik's permission," Jamal said.

"You keep saying that," Cindy exclaimed. "What does he have against me?"

"You could take one of the saddle horses out," Jamal offered, avoiding her question. "The al-Rihanis have only the finest Arabians, you know."

Since it was obviously the only way she could ride until the sheik changed his mind, Cindy accepted Jamal's offer. She selected an athletic-looking bay gelding and quickly tacked him up. She swung onto the saddle and adjusted her stirrups while the horse stood, quiet but alert, waiting for her cues.

They rode by the track as the exercise riders were leading their horses back to the barn. Cindy guided the gelding onto the empty track and began jogging him on the oval. The horse was responsive and willing, although he didn't have the drive of a track-trained Thoroughbred. But after a couple of circuits, Cindy found herself crouched over his shoulders, pushing him to an easy gallop. The Arabian gelding's strides were short and quick, different from those of the leggy racehorses she was used to. The breeze on her face felt wonderful, and she found herself smiling as the bay circled the oval, galloping easily along the rail. When she finally pulled him to a stop, Jamal was standing near the track, a look of surprise on his face.

"He usually fights at the gallop," the barn manager said, sounding impressed. "But he certainly went well for you." He frowned thoughtfully.

"Of course he did," Cindy said, patting the horse's sweaty neck. "Now that you've seen me ride, will you let me work with the colts on the track?"

Jamal shrugged. "The sheik makes the orders," he said. "I just carry them out." He paused, looking at the bay gelding again. "But he will be visiting the stables this afternoon if you wish to discuss it with him then."

"Yes, I definitely do," Cindy said.

When the sheik came down to the barn later that day, Cindy had Champion standing outside his stall, waiting for the sheik's inspection. Sheik al-Rihani strode past the other two stallions and walked straight to Champion. Cindy and Kalim had groomed the stallion to perfection in anticipation of the sheik's visit. Now she stood by the horse's head, one hand resting on his glistening neck.

"My Champion looks like he is doing well," Sheik al-Rihani said, reaching out to run a hand down the stallion's nose.

Cindy nodded. "He is enjoying all the attention he gets here."

The sheik clasped his hands behind his back and circled Champion slowly, eyeing him thoughtfully. "You are doing a fine job with him," he said finally.

"Now that Champion is doing so well, I have some free time. I would be happy to start exercising some of the racehorses for you," Cindy offered. She held her breath.

The sheik gazed at Champion, then looked at Cindy. "I will consider your request," he said. "Meanwhile, you must devote yourself to Champion's care."

Cindy started to protest that she was already devoted to Champion's care. But before she could make a sound, the sheik turned away and began inspecting his other stallions. Cindy sagged against the stall wall and watched him go.

She looked up to see one of the other grooms watching her. She turned away, wrapping her arms around Champion's neck. "I don't know what I'm doing wrong, boy," she said.

Champion released a gusty sigh, and Cindy reached up to rub the whorl of hair on his forehead. "I know, I know," she murmured. "I won't give up. But I don't even know what the problem is, so it's kind of hard to fix it."

I've been here over a month. I'm still stuck at the rail watching the other exercise riders working the racehorses on the track. They can barely ride. The sheik doesn't even have a real trainer. Jamal doesn't want to hear about how White-brook trains. He says things are different here. But I helped train Champion, and he won the Triple Crown. I was so sure the sheik would be dying for my help. Instead he wants me to stay quiet and just take care of Champion. He doesn't understand how much more I could do. I wish he would give me a chance.

10

TIME IS PASSING SO SLOWLY. I DON'T HAVE ANYTHING TO DO but baby-sit Champion and help Jamal around the barn. Champion and I go for long walks early in the morning, when the air is still cool. When we go by the training track, Champion gets excited, and I know he wants to gallop, but the sheik is afraid something bad might happen that would ruin his plans for Champion to sire a stableful of top-class racehorses for the al-Rihani stables. Champion is going to get fat and lazy, and so am I. It's driving me crazy!

Ben is gone most of the time on business trips with his father. Life here is lonelier than I ever thought it would be. But whenever Dad and Beth call I tell them things are great. I don't want them to worry, and I can't just give up and go home. Champion still needs me.

Kalim came to visit with Cindy every day. She

taught him English, and he tried to help her learn a little Arabic and something about the Arab traditions and customs, but Cindy's progress was frustratingly slow.

"If Ramadan ended in January, then what holiday is starting tomorrow?" she asked Kalim.

"Eid ul-Adha," Kalim said. "The Festival of Sacrifice is always in March."

"I'll never remember them all!" Cindy exclaimed as she opened Champion's stall door.

Kalim stepped inside the stall to set a bucket of fresh water in the corner. The horse shoved his nose in Kalim's direction, and the boy rubbed Champion's neck, murmuring to him in his native tongue.

Champion replied with a soft nicker, and Cindy shook her head, smiling at the sight of the boy and the horse. "Even Champion seems to understand Arabic better than me."

"Champion is a brilliant racehorse," Kalim said, grinning at Cindy, clearly proud of his English.

She wrinkled her nose at him. "You're much better at English than I am at Arabic."

The boy beamed. "I like English," he said.

"Me too," Cindy said dryly as they left Champion's stall.

The sun was breaking the horizon as she left the stallion barn. Cindy stopped to watch the handlers lead the racehorses from their barn, tacked up for the morning works.

One of the grooms led a leggy gray colt toward the training track. The young horse's striking movements caught Cindy's attention. He seemed to float across the ground with long, sweeping strides. His refined head showed much of his Arabian heritage, and Cindy longed to be the one taking him onto the track.

"Wyndrake looks great," she told Jamal, who was overseeing the morning warm-ups. "Would you like me to start working with him? I would love to race him for the sheik."

"His jockey has been selected," Jamal said, pointing at a blond-haired man who was walking toward the training track.

"Who is that?" Cindy asked as the man swung onto Wyndrake's back.

"Patrick Scott," Jamal replied. "He's an Irish jockey who has been racing horses for the bin Faheer stables."

Cindy narrowed her eyes, watching closely as Patrick Scott steered Wyndrake onto the track. "He has a good seat," she commented, focusing on the prancing colt as Patrick jogged him along the rail. "But the sheik knows that I am happy to ride any of his horses."

"The sheik wanted Mr. Scott," Jamal said with a note of finality.

"There you are!"

Cindy turned to see Ben crossing the grounds, dressed in a white polo shirt and tan breeches. She felt her heart speed up a little as he smiled warmly at her. Jamal walked over to the rail, leaving them alone.

"It's been so long since I've seen you," Ben said. "I didn't expect my father to plan so many trips so close together. I hope you don't feel like I've deserted you."

Cindy shifted her gaze from Ben to the horses warming up on the track. "I've managed," she said. "I just wish I could spend more time on horseback."

"But you've been riding," Ben protested. "Jamal said you ride one of the saddle horses almost every day."

"It isn't the same as working with the racehorses," Cindy retorted. "I miss being on the track, Ben. It's like torture for me to stand here watching the exercise riders. I should be out there riding, too."

"I understand," Ben said. "But you've only been here a few months. I'm sure that in time you will convince my father that you deserve to ride the Thoroughbreds."

So the sheik isn't ready to give in yet, Cindy thought, her hope dashed to the dirt once more. She still didn't understand why the sheik was so opposed to her riding, but she was sure he thought that eventually she would give up. He didn't seem to understand that determination and stubbornness helped make a jockey good, and she had plenty of both.

Cindy watched Patrick Scott push Wyndrake to a

gallop. The horse moved beautifully, but she didn't like the way Patrick rode him. Wyndrake didn't seem to need much direction, but the jockey handled the reins roughly, and after a few lengths the colt began to fight his rider.

Cindy frowned as she watched the horse's perfect gait fall apart. *Lighten up on him, you idiot,* she thought as Patrick became even more forceful with the colt.

"Cindy!"

Ben's voice snapped her attention back from the track. She darted an apologetic look at him. "I got distracted watching the horse," she said. "I'm sorry, I didn't hear what you asked."

"I said, my parents have planned an outing to the Nad al-Sheba track next week. Would you like to attend the races with us?"

Cindy gnawed at her lower lip, then nodded. "I'd like that," she said. Spending a day with Ben would be nice. She wished they had more time together, but his father seemed very intent on making sure that Ben was ready to take over the family's investment company.

"I haven't been to the track since I rode Champion there," she commented. "It will be interesting to see it from a spectator's view." *And soon,* she vowed silently, *I'll be riding on it again.* Somehow she was going to find a way to show the sheik just how much she deserved to ride for him.

• • •

A few days later, Cindy stood in the doorway of the racehorse barn, watching Jamal try to saddle Wyndrake. The colt was restrained in the crossties, but he twisted his head around so that he could keep a wild eye on Jamal.

"Let me help you tack him up," Cindy offered as the colt scooted his hips sideways to avoid the saddle Jamal held in his hands.

"Kalim is supposed to be helping me with this colt," Jamal said.

"He's with Champion right now," Cindy replied. "They both seem quite content in each other's company," she added, her attention locked on the colt. "Champion loves Kalim."

"Kalim has developed a special relationship with the horse," Jamal commented, taking another step toward Wyndrake. He raised the saddle, and Wyndrake flattened his ears, raising a hind foot. Then the colt froze, as though he wasn't sure whether to kick at Jamal or let the man near him.

"Is he always this difficult?" Cindy asked.

"Not usually," Jamal said, standing quietly until Wyndrake relaxed his foot and lowered it to the ground. "He does seem to be having an off day. I hope he gets past this soon. The sheik will be disappointed if his favorite colt does not do well on the track."

Cindy wanted to pet the nervous animal and reassure him that things were all right, but she knew better than to step in. Jamal was good with the horses, and he would not appreciate her interference.

He took another slow step toward Wyndrake, who snorted nervously. "I need Kalim's assistance," Jamal said. "Perhaps you can find him?"

"But Kalim is busy, and I'm right here," Cindy said. "I'm used to handling difficult horses." She approached the colt's shoulder, her hand extended. Wyndrake swung his head in her direction, his ears flat against his head. Cindy stood her ground, glaring at the colt's sour expression. "I'm not going to hurt you, fellow," she said calmly. She let him sniff at her fingers, prepared to snatch her hand back if he decided to take a bite at her.

Jamal slipped the saddle onto Wyndrake's back while the colt was distracted by Cindy. "He has been growing more high-strung as we near the day of his first race. But he is normally easy to work with."

"He seems so suspicious," Cindy said, holding out her hand. Wyndrake sniffed it nervously, then rolled his eyes and flung his head up. Cindy stood still, and in a moment the colt lowered his head again, taking in her scent with a cautious snort. When she made no move to touch him, he lipped at her palm.

"Are you looking for treats?" she asked quietly, not attempting to pet the edgy colt.

Jamal grimaced as he tightened the girth. He glanced around as though to be sure no one was within earshot, then he turned to Cindy. "As a rider, Mr. Scott seems a little rough for my taste," he said in a low voice. "But the sheik has chosen him as the horse's jockey."

"So Wyndrake is the only horse the sheik is running at Nad al-Sheba?"

Jamal nodded. "Up until a few days ago, I was sure the colt was ready. Now I think my judgment was wrong. I am not an experienced trainer. But Mr. Scott has assured the sheik that Wyndrake has the ability to win his first race." Jamal frowned deeply. "I think Mr. Scott should not be making such claims." He eyed the colt, frowning deeply.

Cindy nodded as Wyndrake allowed her to run a hand lightly along his shoulder. "A horse who is afraid isn't going to run well."

"The bin Faheer manager insists that Mr. Scott is a good jockey," Jamal said, letting Cindy release the crossties. "I would not take it upon myself to change the sheik's mind."

"And he definitely won't listen to me," Cindy muttered under her breath. Every time she approached Habib al-Rihani about exercise-riding the two-year-olds, he put her off again, reminding her that she had been hired to be Champion's handler.

"I'll take him to the track," she told Jamal, unclipping the colt from the crossties. Wyndrake followed her out of the barn. As she led him toward the training track, she wondered if she dared hop on the colt's back and take him around. She could almost feel the wind in her face. *It wouldn't hurt a thing,* she told herself, turning and gathering the colt's reins, preparing to spring onto his back.

"Hold up there," a voice cried, and Cindy froze. She turned to see Patrick Scott striding across the grounds, his helmet and a riding crop dangling from his hand.

"The grooms don't ride," he said loudly. "An inexperienced rider on an inexperienced horse is a bad combination."

As the man neared, Wyndrake tensed, shying away from the hold Cindy had on him. Cindy barely kept the colt's head, and Patrick Scott reached out to grab the reins from her.

Cindy hissed out a breath, resisting the urge to slap Patrick's hand away from the horse. Inexperienced rider? Her? She clenched her jaw, prepared to inform the other jockey of her own riding credentials, but he crowded her to the side and swung onto the antsy colt's back. Wyndrake tried to scoot out from under him, and Cindy cringed as Patrick dug his heel into the colt's side and pulled his head around, making the horse spin in tiny circles.

"I'll show you how to handle a green horse," he said, smiling down at her from Wyndrake's back.

Cindy's jaw began to ache from how tightly she had her teeth gritted. Before she could open her mouth to tell the jockey off, Patrick guided the agitated colt onto the practice track.

Kalim came out of the stallion barn to stand near her at the rail. "He is a jerk," the boy said, glaring at Patrick.

Cindy stifled a laugh. "You've learned your English well," she said, nodding in agreement. Jamal came out of the barn to join them.

"Kalim," he said, "please get my watch from the office. I left it on my desk." The boy hurried away, and Cindy turned to Jamal.

"He's ruining that colt," Cindy told Jamal. "He doesn't deserve to ride such a talented horse."

Jamal sighed but said nothing. When Wyndrake came around the track, his head was up and his eyes were rolled back. His graceful strides were gone, replaced by a choppy, uneven gait.

Patrick rapped the gray colt's hip with his whip. The running horse tried to shift his hips away from the whip, twisting on the track and rearing up a little. In response, the jockey leaned forward and smacked him on the head with the crop.

"No!" Cindy cried.

Jamal groaned as the colt wheeled around, bucking and kicking. "He does this every time. The jockey says the colt must learn to focus on running."

Cindy let out an exasperated breath. "He needs to trust his rider," she snapped.

The jockey didn't seem to have any trouble staying on the horse, and Cindy wondered if he was deliberately making the colt misbehave in order to show off. Disgusted, she turned away. Kalim was almost to the gap in the rail, holding out his father's stopwatch, when his eyes widened and he froze in his tracks.

Cindy whirled back around in time to see Wyndrake charge the fence, exploding through the wooden rail. In his attempt to get away from his rider, the colt was running blindly. Cindy could see the terror in the runaway horse's eyes, and from the look on Patrick Scott's face, she knew he had lost control. Wyndrake was going to run into whatever was in his way.

Cindy spun around and dove at Kalim, tackling him from the side. They rolled onto the ground, and she felt the sting of dirt smacking her face as Wyndrake's hooves hit the ground inches from her eyes.

The galloping horse headed for the barn with Patrick clinging to his back. Cindy sat up slowly. Her heart thundered uncomfortably in her chest, and her left shoulder ached from landing on it when she hit the ground.

Kalim scrambled to his feet, his eyes wide. Jamal hurried to them and helped Cindy to her feet. She tested her shoulder a little, hoping it was only sore from the fall and that she hadn't reinjured it.

"You could have been terribly hurt," Jamal said to Cindy, helping a visibly shaken Kalim dust dirt from his *dishdashah*.

Cindy shrugged. "It should have been Patrick Scott standing there," she said sourly. "He's ruining that colt, Jamal."

Jamal nodded. "I will attempt to reason with the sheik," he said. "But he is a stubborn man who likes to know that he has made a good decision and that his employees trust him in his judgment. He does not like to think he may have made a mistake."

"So I've noticed," Cindy said. She turned to Kalim. "Are you all right?" she asked.

Kalim nodded silently, still trembling from the near accident.

His father spoke to him in Arabic, and Kalim hurried away.

"He will go brush Wyndrake," Jamal said, stooping to pick up his broken stopwatch.

"I'm going to help him," Cindy said, raising a hand

as Jamal started to protest. "And don't try to stop me."

By the time she reached the barn, Patrick Scott was gone, and Wyndrake was standing in his stall, still saddled and shaking.

With Kalim's help, she calmed the distraught horse. Then they led him out of his stall and walked him up and down the barn until his coat was dry. They worked together grooming the colt and reassuring him. Wyndrake was much calmer by the time they were done with him.

Patrick came back into the barn as Kalim was putting the colt back into his stall. When the man came near, Wyndrake pinned his ears and began to tremble again.

"Good," Patrick said to Kalim. "You got him cleaned up." He pointed at Cindy. "I've decided to lay him off until the race. But you need to make sure he has a harsher bit in." He glared at the colt. "That little snaffle did nothing for him today. I need to get him to listen if we're going to get that win for the sheik." He narrowed his eyes at Cindy. "I don't like to lose."

Cindy glared at him, then turned her attention back to the colt.

That night she sat outside the barn, her diary open on her lap. A tiny crescent moon hung in the black sky, and stars glittered in the distance.

It is strange to think that everyone at Whitebrook can see the same moon and stars I can see. I miss my family and the horses there. I wish Dad was here training Wyndrake. He would never let Patrick Scott on a Whitebrook horse. If only there was a way I could show the sheik that I deserve to ride the colt instead. I wish I knew why he is so against me riding. But I think I do know. It's because I'm a woman. Ben said that the UAE wasn't like the Arab countries that oppress women, but I wonder if anyone has ever told the sheik that. He's still stuck in the dark ages.

11

I'M SUPPOSED TO BE GETTING READY TO GO TO THE RACES.
Jamal said the al-Rihanis always dress up to go to the track. I
only have three dresses, and none of them is very fancy. I
should have bought something new that day I went shopping
with Zahra. I've never had to think about what to wear to the
races. I should be putting on my racing silks, not a dress. But
at least I get to spend the day with Ben. That will be fun.

The Nad al-Sheba racetrack was growing crowded
when the limousine driver dropped the al-Rihanis at
the entrance. Ben stayed close to Cindy's side as they
made their way through the grandstand. She could
feel the race-day buzz in the air, and she was trying to
get in the mood to watch the races. But all she really
wanted was to be with the jockeys in the locker room,
preparing to race.

As she eyed the people filling the busy grandstand, Cindy was glad she had decided to wear her blue-and-white calf-length sheath. Most of the other women at the track were also wearing dresses, and Cindy felt she fit in. Zahra was wearing a brightly colored silk dress and a large straw hat.

"You look like you belong in Kentucky on Derby Day," Cindy told her.

Zahra reached up to touch the hat and smiled brightly. "I expect we will be attending some of your American races," she said. "If things go the way Habib hopes, he will have horses running in the Triple Crown races before long."

Ben gave his mother an amused look, then winked at Cindy. "She doesn't have much interest in the horses while they're at home," he said. "But she does love to watch them race, don't you, Mother?"

"I find the horses much more exciting to watch when I can enjoy the comforts of the viewing box," Zahra admitted.

"Don't you want to go down to the stables and see your horse before the race?" Cindy asked, gazing with longing at the end of the track where the stables were located.

"No!" Zahra exclaimed. "All that stomping and snorting and tail swishing makes me nervous." She gave a tiny shudder. "And the smells and dust are overwhelming." She rested her hand lightly on Cindy's arm. "You are a much stronger person than I am to put up with it."

"I don't put up with it," Cindy said, surprised. "I love the smells and the sounds and the work. There is no place as wonderful as a barn!"

She fell silent when the sheik gave her a curious look. He shook his head slightly, then led the way to the family's private viewing box.

Ben leaned close to Cindy as they followed his parents. "My father doesn't understand how a young woman can have such passion for working with horses," he murmured. "He is surprised that you don't want to marry and start a family."

Cindy felt her jaw drop. "Is that the only reason why he won't let me ride?" she demanded, glaring at the sheik's back. "Because I'm a woman and I'm not supposed to be working with the horses?"

Ben nodded slightly. "But I think you're winning him over," he said. "He has commented several times on how well you handle Champion, and he's seen you riding the saddle horses. I'm sure that, given time, you'll change his mind."

"I hope so," Cindy said, following Ben into the al-Rihanis' viewing box. She settled on a soft chair with a perfect view of the track, but it felt so detached from the action below. She wanted to leave the luxurious suite and stand at the rail. Even if she couldn't be racing, she could at least be closer to the horses. But she sat quietly and said nothing.

When the first of the races was called, Cindy grew more glum with each passing moment. Zahra glanced at her, smiling happily. "Isn't this much nicer than being down on the track?" she asked.

Cindy stared down at the starting gate. Nine Thoroughbreds were being loaded for the first race, and Cindy watched with envy as the jockeys sat easily on their prancing mounts, settling into position when the horses were closed into the gate.

In her mind Cindy went back to the night she had ridden Champion to victory in the Dubai Cup. The artificial lights had cast an eerie brightness on the track, and she could feel Champion shifting beneath her, impatient to leave the gate. Even though she had ridden dozens of races since then, nothing had ever compared to the way she had felt in the moments before the Dubai Cup began. And now here she was, back in Dubai with Champion. But while Champion seemed to be content with his new life, hers was nothing like what she had planned.

"That rider in the orange-and-red silks looks nice," Zahra said, leaning close to Cindy.

"He has a good seat," Cindy agreed.

Zahra shook her head. "I meant the colors work well against the gray of his horse."

Cindy winced inwardly. She forced a polite smile for Zahra and turned her attention back to the track.

When the gates banged open for the first race, Cindy imagined how the powerful surge of the horses plunging onto the track felt, and she ached to be among them.

She caught her breath, her whole body tense as she recalled the sensation of those first few seconds of a race. She thought about Ashleigh, astride Limitless Time, racing against her in the Dubai Cup, and how close the race had been. Cindy felt her hands squeeze into fists, as though she had Champion's reins in them and could feel his forceful tug on the bit.

Suddenly the crowd roared as the winner of the first race crossed the finish line. Cindy was jolted back to reality. She hadn't even noticed how the race had been run, let alone who had won.

"Would you like some lemonade?" Zahra asked, touching her arm.

Cindy shook her head. "No, thank you," she said politely, gazing longingly at the track. The only thing she wanted was to be out there on a horse.

When Wyndrake's race was called, Cindy watched Patrick Scott jog the colt onto the track. The gray horse was wired, dancing along the rail and fighting the pony rider, his neck lathered in sweat. When he balked at the gate, Cindy shook her head grimly. It was obvious Wyndrake was upset, and she was sure Patrick was to blame.

"He is handling the colt well," Sheik al-Rihani said.

Cindy closed her eyes and pinched her lips shut. The sheik wasn't going to listen to her, and it was too late now, anyway.

When the race began, Cindy watched Patrick closely, prepared to critique every move he made. But in the first few furlongs the blond jockey skillfully maneuvered the colt through the crush of horses flying around the track, and Cindy could see nothing obvious to complain about. Then she noticed how choppy and rough Wyndrake's stride was, and she groaned to herself. The colt had so much more potential than the jockey was bringing out, and he clearly had the heart to win if he was doing this well despite his distrust of his jockey.

The colt came in third, much to Cindy's surprise. But if she had been riding, he could have won.

"Mr. Scott did an excellent job," the sheik said. "But I am disappointed in the horse," he added, leaning back in his chair. "According to Jamal, the colt had such promise, but his performance today was less than impressive. I don't know that we will bother much more with him."

"Let me work with him," Cindy said eagerly.

The sheik narrowed his eyes and shook his head. "If Mr. Scott cannot get him to run, I am sure you couldn't do better."

Cindy was about to fire back a response, but she clamped her mouth shut. There were so many great races run in Dubai, and she didn't intend to give up her only chance of riding in them. She had to figure out a way to make Sheik al-Rihani see that she was worthy of racing his Thoroughbreds.

That evening, when she returned to the stables, she let herself into Champion's stall. She glanced at his water bucket to see if it needed filling, but it was filled to the rim with cool, fresh water. She caught a faint whiff of apple when Champion shoved his nose at her.

"Kalim spoils you, doesn't he?" she commented, petting Champion's sleek neck. "So you won't mind if I spend some time working with another horse, will you?" Champion nickered softly when she rested her cheek against his shoulder. "Good," she said. "Because now that I know you're happy here, boy, I need to do a few things for myself."

Champion seems very content, and Kalim loves him as much as I do. I need to make the sheik see that I can ride bet-

ter than any of the jockeys here. I didn't realize this kind of ignorance existed in this day and age. I guess I've taken my freedom for granted. But Ben is more open-minded, and he says women in the UAE are free to do as they wish. So it's not against the law or anything. I want to be a jockey here, and I'm not going home without at least trying. I'm going to convince the sheik to let me ride—if it's the last thing I do.

126

12

BEN PROMISED THAT WHEN HE GOT BACK FROM HIS NEXT TRIP *we would spend a day exploring Dubai. So that's what we're doing today. He says he's taking me to the camel races, which should be pretty funny.*

It's almost the middle of May. I can't believe I've been here four months. And I'm still not allowed to ride any of the Thoroughbreds. I don't know what to do.

"You were serious about the camel races," Cindy exclaimed, gawking at the scene before them as Ben parked his Land Rover. Men were leading their huge, awkward mounts over to the track to race. And hordes of people spilled out of large, colorfully decorated tents. The cries of food vendors and bawling camels filled the air.

"First we'll go to the *souq*," Ben said, nodding

toward the large, open-air marketplace. "Then we'll see the camels run."

They crossed the parking lot, and Cindy could see the rows of stalls that the vendors had set up, selling everything from vegetables to hand-woven carpets. Canopies were draped over the wide aisles to give some relief from the sun. They joined other shoppers walking between the rows of booths.

A group of boys darted around them, laughing and shouting as they raced through the market. Ben caught Cindy by the arm as one of the boys ran into her.

"Are you all right?" he asked, steadying her as the startled boy dashed off to join his friends.

"Of course," Cindy said. "I'm used to being pushed around by thousand-pound horses, remember?"

Ben nodded. "When you are standing beside me you seem so small. It is hard to remember that you are used to controlling Thoroughbreds on the racetrack."

Cindy wrinkled her nose. "I'm having a little trouble remembering that myself," she said. "I don't think your father is ever going to let me race one of his horses."

Ben sighed. "He's a very traditional man," he said. "It is still a struggle for him to accept the changes he has seen in his lifetime." He offered Cindy an encouraging smile. "But he'll come around. Just give him more time." A band of musicians was playing under a canopy, filling the air with the haunting sounds of traditional Arab music. For a moment Cindy felt as if she had been transported back in time. "I keep expecting to see someone fly by on a magic carpet," she joked to Ben.

He laughed. "Come," he said, pointing toward the busy stalls. "Let's see if we can find your magic carpet."

Spending time alone with Ben was fun. Cindy let him lead her to the first booth, where scarves of all colors of the rainbow were on display. Ben picked out a pristine white rectangle of cloth and paid for it, then tucked the neatly wrapped package under his arm as they headed on through the noisy, crowded rows of booths.

They passed stands filled with trays of shimmering gold jewelry, stacks of hand-woven baskets, and colorful displays of fresh vegetables. They stopped at a food vendor's cart and bought a meal of pita bread stuffed with spicy chickpea filling, and bottles of fruit juice.

As they ate, Cindy gazed around, trying to take in everything she hadn't seen yet.

"Look at that," Cindy said, pointing at a nearby booth.

"Traditional Arab horse tack," Ben said.

Cindy hurried to the shop, with Ben behind her. "Look at the tassels on the breast collar," she said, holding up a colorful piece.

"That's called a *shoband*," Ben said.

"And this?" Cindy said, pointing at a lead rope.

"*Megwad*," Ben said. "And this is called *egal*," he added, picking up a headstall.

Cindy picked out several pieces of tack, including a saddle made of embroidered velvet. "I don't know when I'll use these, but they'll be great to have," she said, paying for her purchases.

"Then we shall put these in the car and go watch the camel races," Ben said.

"This is fun," Cindy told him as they stowed her new treasures in the car.

"I'm glad," Ben said, smiling warmly. "I enjoy being with you."

Cindy felt her face grow hot under his gaze, and she smiled back. "I like being with you, too," she said.

Ben led her to a row of seats beneath a canopy, and they watched the camels line up for their race. When Ben leaned close to her, Cindy felt her heart speed up. She caught a whiff of his cologne, and she inhaled deeply, trying to lock the scent in her mind.

She wondered at herself. She had never felt like this before. She got a little light-headed whenever he looked at her, and a little breathless whenever he leaned close to her. *It must be the heat getting to me*, she told herself, but she knew that wasn't it. She was almost certain she was falling in love with Ben.

"Look at the jockeys," Ben said, pointing toward a group of young boys dressed in brightly colored traditional Arab clothing.

Cindy gawked at the sight of the riders pulling on Velcro-seated overpants. "Why are they wearing those?" she asked.

"The camels have matching pads on their backs so the jockeys will be able to stay on. They used to tie the riders to the camels, but that is far too dangerous."

Cindy nodded. "There are times when I could use a pair of those," she said. "What a great idea."

When she saw the riders sitting on the camels' sloping backs, behind the humps, she understood why they needed to be attached to their mounts. The camels craned their long necks, swiveling their heads back and forth, bleating loudly as they waited for the start of the race. The creatures looked silly with their big eyes, long lashes, and flat noses, and they walked with a disjointed, rolling gait. They were nothing like racehorses, with their refined heads, alert ears, and graceful gait.

"This is going to be hilarious," she said, imagining how funny the running camels would look.

To her surprise, the odd-looking creatures were fast and moved with far more grace than she had ever dreamed possible. The crowd cheered and shouted as the animals stretched out and galloped, charging for

131

the finish line. Cindy found herself cheering for a light brown camel that took the lead quickly and kept it throughout the race. Cindy grabbed Ben's arm and yelled encouragement, whooping loudly as the animal galloped across the finish line in first place.

When they returned to the villa, Ben parked by the barn. "I thought we could saddle up a couple of the Arabians and ride down to the beach," he said. "We still have plenty of time before the sun sets, if you'd like to go."

"Do you have to ask if I want to go riding?" Cindy said with a smile.

Ben handed her the white scarf he had bought. "Your own *gutrah*," he said. "It will cover your head and protect you from the sun and wind while we ride through the desert."

Cindy draped the scarf on her head, using a metal ring Ben called an *ogal* to fix the head covering in place. She saddled her horse with her new Arabian tack while Ben got an English saddle from the tack room for his horse. When Cindy swung onto her mount's back, she swept the sides of the *gutrah* back from her face and grinned at Ben.

"You look like a Bedouin," Ben said, settling onto his horse's back.

"A blond, blue-eyed Arab?" she asked, laughing.

With Ben in the lead, they rode out of the valley

and across an expanse of rocky soil before reaching a stretch of wind-carved sand.

The horses walked steadily, plodding across the shifting sand. "The desert is so imposing," Cindy said as the horses climbed a rise.

"Yes," Ben said solemnly. "The desert is uncompromising and unforgiving. Much like my father," he added.

Cindy shot him a sharp look, and Ben gave her a crooked smile. "Don't misunderstand," he said quickly. "He is a very good man, but he is a little . . ."

"Stubborn?" Cindy offered.

Ben nodded.

When they reached the top of the dune, Cindy pulled her horse to a stop. The waters of the Persian Gulf shimmered in the afternoon light, and waves lapped at the sandy beach.

"Come," Ben said, urging his horse into a canter. They rode down the low slope and onto the beach. Soon they were galloping along the water's edge, the horses' hooves thudding hollowly on the wet sand, splashing them with salty water. Cindy crouched over the gelding's shoulders and urged him on, laughing as the cool ocean wind swept over her face. She touched her tongue to her lips, tasting the salt from the water's spray.

Long before she was ready to stop, they reined the

horses in. They sat in the shelter of a rocky outcropping while the horses stood by quietly, relaxing in the shadows cast by the rocks in the setting sun.

Cindy sat cross-legged on the sand, watching the magnificent colors that spread across the water. Ben stretched his legs out and leaned back, resting his weight on his elbow.

"Thanks for the great day," Cindy said, glancing over at him.

"I'm so glad you enjoyed yourself," Ben replied, gazing up at her. "I had a wonderful time just being with you."

Cindy felt her face flame at his words, and she jumped to her feet. "I think it's time to go back," she said.

"Yes, I suppose you're right," Ben said a little reluctantly. He rose slowly. "It will be dark soon."

Cindy was quiet on the ride back. The angle of the setting sun created dark lines in the sand, and the air cooled rapidly as the day's heat disappeared.

"What's wrong?" Ben asked, riding beside her. "I thought going for a ride would make you happy."

"It did," Cindy said, forcing herself to smile. "But galloping on the beach just reminded me of how much I miss racing."

"I'll talk to my father about letting you ride the Thoroughbreds," Ben promised.

Cindy nodded, but she didn't think the sheik would change his mind.

Several days later Jamal stood beside Cindy at the rail of the training track, watching the horses being worked. One of the exercise riders galloped by, barely able to keep his seat on the running horse, and Cindy groaned in frustration.

"What am I doing wrong?" she asked Jamal. "My credentials are just as good as those of Patrick Scott or any of these riders, if not better."

"Mr. Scott has won several major races on the international circuit," Jamal said. "The sheik values that."

"But I won the Dubai Cup. How much better could I be?" Cindy demanded.

Jamal pressed his lips together, then turned to Cindy with a pained expression. "The sheik believes that Champion won the Cup in spite of you, not because of your ability."

Cindy felt her jaw drop. "I don't believe it," she said, turning away from Jamal. It didn't matter how many races she'd won, she realized. She was a woman. That was all that mattered to the sheik. If a horse went well for her, he'd see it as luck, not skill.

When Cindy fed Champion that night, she wrapped her arms around the stallion's neck and inhaled his familiar scent. She closed her eyes, pretending she was back in Kentucky for a moment, wishing she could spirit Champion away and take him for a long ride on the wonderful trails around Whitebrook.

"Did you win the Dubai Cup in spite of me, boy?" she asked. "Didn't I ride well?"

Champion nudged her, and Cindy sighed. "You are a fantastic horse," she said. "Maybe I'm not such a hotshot jockey after all." She rubbed her eyes wearily.

Later she sat down in front of Champion's stall with the intention of writing a cheerful letter home. Instead she opened her diary.

The only way I'm ever going to know if I'm a good jockey or if I've just been lucky enough to have good horses is to race again. And without the sheik's permission, that isn't likely to happen while I'm living here. I don't know what I can do to change things. Maybe I should just go home.

13

IT HAS BEEN TWO WEEKS SINCE BEN AND I WENT RIDING ON the beach. I'm so confused. Every time I hear he is leaving for another business trip, I feel so disappointed. If only I could spend more time with him, I wouldn't feel so lonely and restless. I got a letter from Beth yesterday, with pictures of Kevin and Christina sitting on Wonder, and a photo of Samantha and Shining. It's summer now, and Kentucky looks so green and lush compared to the Arabian desert. I really miss Whitebrook and my family.

Jamal didn't say anything when he saw Cindy at Wyndrake's stall every morning, helping Kalim with the high-strung colt. But he still would not allow her to ride the colt. "Not until I have clearance from the sheik," he said. Cindy knew that the sheik wouldn't give in, but neither would she.

One evening she wandered into the stallion barn and let herself into Champion's stall. The horse nickered softly, barely glancing up when she rested her hand on his chestnut-colored shoulder.

She heard Ben's footsteps in the aisle and looked up to smile at him when he stopped in front of Champion's stall.

"You have seemed distracted the last several days," Ben commented, watching Cindy smooth Champion's forelock. The chestnut stallion had his nose buried in a pan full of apple slices that Kalim had left for him. Cindy knew Champion was behaving as well for Kalim as he ever had for her, and she felt a little useless, although she was happy that someone else loved the big stallion as much as she did.

She darted a quick smile at Ben. "I'm fine," she said. "I guess I'm just a little homesick."

"What would make you smile again?" Ben asked.

Cindy looked at him boldly. "Galloping Wyndrake," she said. "I want to take him onto the track."

Ben raised his eyebrows for a second, then gave her a long, thoughtful look. "Then you shall do it," he said, opening Champion's door and gesturing for her to leave the stall.

Ben led the way to the barn where Wyndrake was kept, walking confidently down the aisle. Cindy hesitated for a fraction of a second, then hurried after Ben.

Wyndrake nickered softly when he saw her, and Cindy clipped a lead line on the colt's halter. He followed her willingly to the crossties in the middle of the barn. She felt strange, sneaking around the barn as though she were some sort of criminal. If the sheik found out, he would probably send her packing, and she'd never see Champion, or Ben, again.

"I'll get fired if your father finds out," she said.

Ben shook his head. "I'll tell him I ordered you to do it," he said. "I will be responsible."

"That isn't right," Cindy protested. "Besides, he'd never believe it."

But the longing to ride on the track was so strong that she couldn't ignore it. She wasn't going to get caught, she reassured herself. At this time of the evening the staff had all gone home, Jamal would be in his small house with his family, eating dinner, and Ben's parents were at a dinner party. She was perfectly safe.

"Get a saddle," Ben said, picking up a brush.

Cindy paused for only a second before she hurried to the tack room to get the equipment. She was reaching for a bridle when she heard footsteps in the aisle. She froze, her hand on the headstall, her heart in her throat.

"What are you doing?"

She turned slowly to face Jamal. The barn manager

stood in the doorway, his hands propped on his hips. She could barely see his face in the low light, but she was pretty sure he wasn't smiling.

She worked her jaw, trying to think of a believable excuse, but she couldn't bring herself to lie to Jamal.

"I'm going to ride Wyndrake," she said flatly. "Please, Jamal," she added desperately. "I know you need to report this to the sheik, but at least wait until after I've ridden him."

The barn manager's face was stern as he considered what she had said. Cindy held her breath, waiting.

Then Jamal's shoulders relaxed. "I'll get his bridle," he said.

Cindy grabbed a saddle and dashed back to where Ben was brushing the colt. By the time Cindy and Ben had the saddle in place, Jamal had brought the bridle and a stopwatch.

He shrugged when Cindy looked at the watch. "I, too, would like to see what you can do with this colt," he said.

The lights in the stable area lit their path to the track. Cindy hesitated by the opening in the rail.

"Do I have to order you to ride?" Ben asked in a teasing voice.

Cindy looked from Wyndrake to the track and then at Ben. "No one ever has to order me to get on a horse!" She popped her helmet on her head. "I'm ready," she said, turning to grab the reins and a handful of the colt's mane.

Wyndrake began to tremble as Cindy rode him onto the track. She held him to a walk and reached down to gently stroke his neck. "It's just me, boy," she murmured, despising Patrick Scott for his heavy hands and aggressive riding. She kept the colt to the rail and walked him slowly, uttering reassurances as they circled the track. By the time they finished a slow circuit, Wyndrake was much calmer.

Feeling confident about her ability to handle the colt, Cindy urged him into a trot. Wyndrake flung his head high and skittered across the track, nervously flicking his ears back and forth. It was as though he was waiting for Patrick's whip to fall.

Cindy kept him moving steadily forward. "We're alone out here, Wyndrake," she said in a calm voice, reminding the colt that it was her on his back. "Just the two of us. No one is going to hurt you. Don't be afraid. You're perfectly safe now."

Slowly the colt began to lower his head and lengthen his strides. Cindy bit down the urge to whoop with elation as Wyndrake moved into a long, smooth trot.

By the time she turned him to gallop counterclockwise, the colt was warmed up and eager to run. Now the humming she felt in his muscles was energy, not fear. She grinned to herself, feeling the restrained power in the Thoroughbred's tense muscles. "Let's do it, boy," she said, crouching over his shoulders.

Wyndrake broke into a strong gallop, and Cindy felt her heart soar. This was it—this was what she had been missing, what she had been waiting so long for. "Come on, boy!" she cried, and Wyndrake stretched out, thundering along the rail as though he were heading for the finish line at Churchill Downs. The furlongs passed quickly, and after she had counted half a mile, Cindy reluctantly brought the colt around.

As they returned to the gap in the rail, she felt her joy fade a little. Was she going to have to skulk around the practice track at night in order to ride? She reached down to pat Wyndrake's shoulder. "You're an awesome horse," she said. "You deserve a much better jockey than Patrick Scott. All this sneaking around is unfair to you . . . and to me."

When she reached Jamal and Ben, both men were staring at her, wide-eyed.

Ben shook his head. "That cannot be the same horse that ran so awkwardly at the track two weeks ago," he said. "His strides are completely different."

"He works well for a more skilled jockey," Cindy said smartly, hopping from the colt's back.

Jamal held out the stopwatch. "Look at these fractions," he said.

Cindy glanced at the watch and shrugged. "I knew he felt fast," she said, turning to rub the colt's sweaty shoulder. "And I know he can do even better than that. We were just getting a feel for each other, weren't we, boy?"

Jamal gave Cindy a hard look. "With you riding this colt, he could win the Godolphin Mile."

"But without the sheik's okay, I'll never get to ride him," Cindy retorted.

Jamal frowned. "I will try to reason with him," he said. "I will do my best."

Impulsively Cindy flung her arms around the barn manager's neck. "Thank you!" she cried.

Jamal stepped back and quickly took Wyndrake. "I will cool him out," he said, striding away with the prancing colt.

Ben looked down at Cindy and smiled. "It's back," he said, nodding approvingly. He touched her cheek with his fingertip.

"What?" Cindy asked, blushing self-consciously. "What's back?"

"Your smile," Ben said, lightly stroking her cheek. "Many times since you have been here, I have seen you form your lips into a smile. Now your smile is back in your eyes. That is what has been missing." He frowned thoughtfully. "You are right," he said. "You do need to be on the racehorses. For you not to race is like not allowing a dolphin to swim. My father does not understand that. I need to make him see it." He rubbed his chin with his thumb. "I will find a way. I promise."

For the next several days Cindy worked with Wyndrake while Kalim took care of Champion. Jamal allowed her to take the colt onto the track when none of the other exercise riders was around. Cindy hated lurking around waiting for chances to work with the colt, but it was worth it. He grew calmer and more willing every time she saddled him and rode him onto the practice track. Given the chance, the colt would be a fantastic sprinter, but without the right jockey, he would never be first-rate.

"Will you speak to Sheik al-Rihani soon?" she asked Jamal. "It would be so much better for Wyndrake to work while there are other horses on the track. I don't like prowling around, hiding what I'm doing."

Jamal sighed. "Right now the sheik is busy planning a local competition among a few of his friends. I have not been able to get him to sit down and discuss Wyndrake."

"What kind of competition?" Cindy asked curiously.

"A horse race, of course," Jamal said. "Here, on the practice track."

He shook his head before Cindy could say anything. "He will not run Wyndrake," he said. "I did ask him that, and he feels the colt would embarrass him with another inferior performance."

Cindy bristled. "That colt is the most talented runner of all the al-Rihani horses," she exclaimed.

Jamal shrugged. "I agree," he said. "But I am only the sheik's employee. I can make suggestions, but I cannot force him to change his mind."

Cindy went back to work, her jaw clenched with frustration. She started for Champion's stall but saw Kalim there with the big stallion and hesitated. The boy spent so much time with Champion, it seemed that he was more Kalim's responsibility than hers. She turned and walked away, going instead to Wyndrake's stall to groom the gray colt.

The next morning when Cindy led Wyndrake out of the barn, tacked for his daily work, she saw the sheik coming down the path toward the barns. This was her chance, she realized. Jamal must have asked him to come down so that he could see her ride. Now she could show the sheik just how well Wyndrake could perform!

"It's you and me, boy," Cindy told the colt, who looked at the track with sharply pointed ears and flared nostrils. "Do you want to go work out with me? We can show the sheik what we can do together."

The colt pranced a little, snorting with excitement, and Cindy started to gather the reins in her hand.

"There you are!"

Cindy felt her shoulders sag as she heard Patrick Scott's voice. She turned to see the jockey hurrying toward them. "Jamal has convinced the sheik to give this gray another chance on the track," Patrick said. "I am supposed to take him out so the sheik can watch him." The Irishman nudged Cindy aside and checked Wyndrake's girth.

Cindy curled her lip, wanting to snap at him that she knew how to tack up a horse. Before she could say anything Patrick took the reins from her, vaulted onto Wyndrake's back, and rode away, leaving Cindy speechless.

Jamal joined the sheik at the practice track as Patrick started to warm Wyndrake up. Cindy stood back, watching for Wyndrake's smooth gait to fall apart. But the work she had been doing with the colt seemed to be staying with him. When Patrick moved Wyndrake into a gallop, the sheik nodded approvingly. "We will give him another chance," he said to Jamal. "I want Patrick to race him again."

Cindy started to take a step forward, ready to tell the sheik who had helped Wyndrake. But she caught herself. If Sheik al-Rihani knew Jamal had been letting her work the colt, the barn manager might lose his job. She bit her tongue and wheeled away, furious and frustrated.

That evening, after she got ready for bed, she opened her diary. She wrote so hard that the pen dug into the paper, tearing the page.

I can't believe the sheik thinks Champion won the Dubai Cup in spite of me. If he found out I've been riding Wyndrake, would he say Wyndrake was going well in spite of me, too? Now Patrick Scott is going to ride Wyndrake and ruin all my hard work. If I could just find a way to show the sheik I can ride . . .

*I WONDER WHAT DAD WOULD SAY IF I TOLD HIM WHAT WAS
really going on. He'd probably say that I should have listened to him. I've been telling everyone at Whitebrook how
great things are going. I was so sure my jockey career was
going to take off here.*

*If I leave, I'll never see Champion again, and every time
I look at Ben I feel like I want to be around him all the time.
But without being able to do what I love, I feel so lost. I am
so confused.*

On the day of the al-Rihanis' race, Cindy spent the
morning helping Kalim set up the spectators' area by
the practice track. They hung bunting and brightly colored banners from the light poles and soon had the
small track looking festive for the visitors.

When they were done, Cindy stepped back to view

their handiwork. The colorful banners stirring in the soft desert breeze seemed to mock her somber mood, but she forced a smile for Kalim. "We did a great job," she said. "It looks perfect, Kalim."

"This will be an exciting evening," Kalim said, admiring the track.

"I'm sure the al-Rihanis and their guests will have a wonderful time," Cindy said, gazing at the starting gate, which a man was oiling. Another man was dragging the track with a large tractor, smoothing the footing for the horses. It would all be very exciting and lots of fun for the guests—and for her, too, if she could have been a part of it.

"But you will be there, right?" Kalim asked, giving her a concerned look.

Cindy smiled at the boy and shook her head. "I don't think I can bear to sit on the sidelines and watch," she said. "I'm probably not being a very good sport, but it just isn't fair that I'm not being allowed to ride."

"You wish to race," Kalim said in an understanding voice.

Cindy nodded sadly. "More than anything," she said.

When the first horse van arrived, Cindy went to her room in the grooms' quarters and picked up her diary. She would have loved to see the different horses being brought to the estate, and talk to the trainers and jockeys, but what was the point?

She tried to shake her gloomy mood by reminding herself that Ben was on her side. Only he obviously wasn't making any more progress with his father than Jamal had. Here was another opportunity to prove herself, but she wasn't being given a chance.

She left her room, too restless to stay inside and write. No one else was in the stallion barn, and she strolled down the quiet aisle, barely glancing at the sheik's other stallions. When she reached Champion's stall, the stallion had his head down and his eyes half closed. She stood outside the stall for a moment, admiring the horse's magnificent build and the shape of his perfectly formed head. Even relaxed in the shadows, Champion was an imposing sight.

When she let herself into the stall, the big chestnut stallion flicked his ears in her direction. He lifted his head and whooshed air from his nostrils, then nickered softly to her. Cindy cupped his jaw in her hands and pressed her cheek against his forehead.

"I'm so glad you're content here," she said to him, feeling the smooth warmth of his coat under her hands. "Things aren't going quite the way I had planned for me, though," she added. Champion nuzzled her, and Cindy gently massaged the base of his ears until the stallion lowered his head again. His lower lip went slack as he relaxed, and Cindy smiled in spite of herself. "I love you, Champion," she said softly. "No matter what else happens here, I'll know that you're safe and well cared for."

Cindy was determined not to go out to the track, but when it started to get dark, she left Champion's stall. Her feet seemed to have a mind of their own, and she started walking toward the track. She knew it would only torment her to watch Patrick Scott ride Wyndrake, but she couldn't stay away from the horses. Even if she couldn't ride, she wanted to see how Wyndrake ran against the small field of horses. At least then she would know she had helped the colt run better, even if no one else would acknowledge her work.

She could see the lights glowing over the practice track. It brought back the memory of racing Champion in the Dubai Cup, only the memory didn't bring back that glorious feeling of elation she had experienced on the track. It wasn't just luck and a good horse that had won that race for her. She had ridden well. She was a good jockey, she reassured herself. But the voice in her mind didn't seem to carry much strength anymore. The sheik didn't think she was good enough to ride his horses, and unless she had a chance to test herself against a field of good horses and jockeys, she'd never know if he was right or if she was.

When she started to pass the racehorse barn, a movement in the shadow of the building made her jump. She spun to face Kalim, who stepped away from the building and gestured at her.

Cindy frowned at the boy, who looked around anxiously before he took another step closer to her. He held an armful of clothing, with a racing helmet perched on top of the pants and shirt.

"You must change quickly," he said, thrusting the bundle of clothes at her. Then he hurried away, disappearing into the racehorse barn. Cindy stared after him for a few seconds, then shrugged. She didn't know who had decided to let her ride, but she wasn't about to question her good fortune.

She slipped into the tack room and quickly changed into the al-Rihani silks, tugging on a pair of boots that were a tight fit, but she forced her feet into them. Ill-fitting boots were not going to come between her and the track.

Once she was dressed, she paused to look down at herself, amazed at how good it felt to be dressed in racing silks after so many months. For the first time in ages, Cindy felt as though everything was all right.

She headed down the barn aisle, whistling softly to herself, the helmet tucked under her arm. She hesitated when she saw Wyndrake standing in the crossties, wearing the racing saddle her parents had given her for her eighteenth birthday. Kalim stood at the colt's head, looking tense.

"Hurry," he said in a hushed voice.

"Where's Patrick Scott?" Cindy asked, glancing around the quiet barn. "Did something happen to him? He is supposed to be racing Wyndrake."

Kalim shook his head. "Your ride," he said, nodding toward Wyndrake. Cindy narrowed her eyes at the boy. "Are you sure about this?" she asked. She wanted to race badly enough to do just about anything, but she didn't want anyone else getting in trouble for it.

"Is Patrick all right?" she demanded. "Is he sick? Did the sheik say I was supposed to ride?"

Kalim shrugged and said something in Arabic.

"Oh," Cindy said, giving the boy a hard look. "All those months of English lessons and now you don't understand me?"

Kalim ignored her. Instead he unclipped the colt from the crossties and led him from the barn.

Cindy hesitated for only a second before she followed Kalim and Wyndrake outside. If there was a miscommunication, it wasn't her fault. She was going to ride Wyndrake in front of the sheik and show him just what a talented horse he was—and what a talented rider she was.

She pulled on her helmet and realized that with the

153

distance from the spectators' area to the gate, if the sheik saw a blond rider on Wyndrake, he would assume it was Patrick. She glanced around one more time, curious as to the whereabouts of the missing jockey. But Patrick was nowhere to be seen. Cindy hurried after Kalim and Wyndrake, who were almost to the starting gate. When they reached the chute, four other horses were already there, their jockeys already mounted and waiting behind the gate. Handlers stood at each horse's head, keeping the Thoroughbreds under control until they were to be loaded into their slots.

In the brightly decorated spectators' area, Cindy could see the figures of the al-Rihanis and their guests, standing at the rail, talking and gesturing. The group looked as though they were having a great time, but Cindy was thrilled to be sitting on a horse instead of standing at the rail watching the horses go by.

Ben was at his father's side, gazing intently toward the gate. Cindy could see him squint in her direction, but with all the horses and people milling around, she doubted he would be able to tell whether it was her or Patrick Scott. She swallowed around a lump of nerves that had suddenly formed in her throat. She wasn't supposed to be doing this, she was certain of that, but she couldn't stop herself. This was where she belonged.

She turned back to the track, and Kalim gave her a leg up. They took their place behind the number five gate. Jamal was at the gate controls next to the number one slot. Cindy kept her face turned away from the barn manager. She didn't know what he would do if he realized she was riding the colt, and she didn't want to find out.

When Jamal gestured for the riders to enter the gate, Kalim directed Wyndrake into his narrow slot. Cindy ignored the glares of the jockey to her left. She was finally going to race in Dubai again, and nothing was going to spoil it for her.

She settled onto the saddle, shifting her weight and adjusting the reins in her hands. When she looked over the gate at the stretch of dirt track in front of her, her heart sped up. A tingling sensation coursed through her, making her fingertips hum with electricity. She patted Wyndrake's sleek shoulder and took a deep breath. This was it!

Jamal spoke loudly, and the group at the rail fell silent, focusing their attention on the gate.

Beneath Cindy, Wyndrake snorted softly. "This is a chance for both of us, boy," she murmured, giving his neck a pat. "Six furlongs. Nothing to it, right? Let's just burn up the track and leave them all wondering what happened." She had never ridden Wyndrake with other horses on the track. She had only seen him come out of the gate at the Nad al-Sheba track. Then it had appeared that he didn't like the horses around him, and when he couldn't plunge ahead to get out of the crush, he had slowed down to avoid being caught in the traffic.

"I'll try to keep you happy out there," she muttered, giving him one more pat for reassurance.

Wyndrake shifted and tensed, and Cindy crouched over his neck. She gripped the reins tightly and pressed her toes against the stirrups. Her heart drummed so loudly that she was sure Jamal must be able to hear it at the other end of the gate. But it was excitement, not fear, that she was feeling. It felt so right to be on the colt's back, anticipating the explosive beginning of the race.

Jamal yelled something in Arabic, and Cindy tangled some of Wyndrake's mane in her fingers, bracing for the start.

Then the gate snapped open, and the horses surged onto the track in a thundering wave. *Six furlongs*, Cindy reminded herself, angling Wyndrake toward the inside of the oval.

The field crowded around them, and Cindy felt Wyndrake tense. His head flew up as the running horses enveloped him.

"Easy!" Cindy cried. She leaned forward and rubbed her knuckles against his neck. "It's okay," she called to the tense colt. "It's me you're running for. I know what you need. Trust me, boy. I'll get you out of this. Come on, we can do this!"

Wyndrake angled his ears back, listening to her, and his neck relaxed a little. Cindy maneuvered him toward a tiny hole between two chestnut horses, and Wyndrake dove for the opening, intent on getting to the empty stretch of track beyond the other horses.

She had figured him out, Cindy realized with a surge of relief. Wyndrake flew past another gray colt, galloping strongly beneath her. Now they were in second place. Cindy eased the colt over to the rail, urgently aware that each fraction of a second brought them closer to the finish line, which was coming up fast. In two strides they caught up with the bay colt that had been in the number one slot.

"We're out of time!" she shouted to Wyndrake, taking up a bit more rein. In response, the colt leaned into the bit and sped up, devouring the track with his huge strides.

Cindy's heart soared. She and Wyndrake were going to win this together!

As they thundered past the lead horse Cindy heard the pounding of hooves coming up beside them. They bore down on the finish line, and when Wyndrake crossed it they were alone, a full length ahead of the second-place horse. Cindy let out a whoop of joy, raising her fisted hand in the air as she stood up in the stirrups. She felt a broad grin splitting her face. Now the sheik would have to admit that she could handle the competition. He would have no reason not to allow her to race after this!

She slowed Wyndrake to a jog and turned him back, eager to ride past the sheik and his company so that he could acknowledge his winning colt.

But she sank onto the saddle when she saw the group of spectators staring in her direction. There wasn't a smiling face among them except for Ben's. Patrick Scott was standing beside Sheik al-Rihani, glaring at her, and the sheik was wearing the darkest frown Cindy had ever seen.

I thought the sheik was going to explode. Instead he was very quiet, and told me he would discuss the race with me later. Then everyone went back to the house, including Ben. He didn't even say a word to me. I need to get out of here. Champion may be right at home here, but I don't belong in Dubai.

15

I've been sitting here for hours. I feel like I'm waiting to hear what my punishment will be. This is crazy. I should just quit before the sheik comes down and fires me.

When a knock sounded on the door, she rose slowly and opened it, surprised to see Ben standing there instead of his father. "What a race," he said, grinning at her. "You showed them all, didn't you?"

Cindy grimaced. "I thought if your father saw me ride, he would have to change his mind about letting me race, but I guess he wasn't so happy that I did it behind his back."

Ben's smile faded and he nodded. "He felt that you embarrassed him in front of his friends," he said. "But you rode so well." He smiled again. "Cindy, you were fantastic. You and Wyndrake both made it look so

159

easy. Even my father had to admit that you handled the horse with far more skill than Patrick Scott."

"Like that does me any good," Cindy said flatly.

"But he saw it," Ben said. "We all did. You belong in the saddle."

"It's too bad you don't run the stables," Cindy said.

"Yes," Ben said. "I would certainly do things differently." He sighed. "Right now I need to return to the house, but I wanted to tell you how magnificent you were with Wyndrake."

After Ben left, Cindy stood in the doorway, trying to figure out what to do. She didn't remember ever feeling this miserable before. Letting Ben and Jamal try to reason with the sheik on her behalf had done her absolutely no good, and obviously sneaking around had been a huge mistake.

Cindy started after Ben. She had no reason to hide from the sheik. He was in the wrong, not she. She headed for the house as the last of the visitors' cars left the driveway.

When she came around the corner of the barn, she saw Ben and his father standing in the glow of the vapor light near the barn door. The sheik had his arms folded across his chest. Cindy hesitated in the shadows.

"I cannot tolerate that kind of behavior," the sheik said. "I cannot let a young woman humiliate me before my friends."

"She won the race for you," Ben said.

"But everyone was aware that she was riding without my permission," the sheik said. "How can I expect respect from my peers when a young woman is allowed to show me such disdain?"

"They knew only because Patrick Scott complained so loudly to you that everyone heard," Ben said.

Cindy grimaced, wondering who had kept Patrick away from the track long enough for him to miss the race.

"He had every right," the sheik retorted. "I hired him to ride the horse. Her behavior was inappropriate, and if I allow this to go without a reprimand, I will no longer have the respect of my employees."

"I understand, Father," Ben said. "A woman's place is not on the track. Cindy had no business competing with the men. It was a terrible humiliation that she rode better than all of the men."

"I am glad you see things my way," the sheik said, clapping his hand on Ben's shoulder.

Cindy sagged against the barn wall, unable to believe what she was hearing Ben say.

"Cindy never should have taken Wyndrake onto the track," Ben continued. "Protecting your dignity is more important than the fact that she won the race."

"That is exactly how I feel," the sheik said firmly.

Before she could hear any more, Cindy turned away.

She found Jamal in his office, staring at the wall, his face creased deeply with a frown. "It was my doing," he said. "I set things up so that you could race. I know the sheik is outraged, and I should accept the blame."

"It wasn't your fault!" Cindy exclaimed, shaking her head. She sank onto a chair near the door and added more quietly, "But I am going to leave now. I can't stay here."

"I understand," Jamal said. "What do you plan to do?"

Cindy pressed her lips together in a determined line. "I think I'll go to New York for a while," she said. "I know some of the trainers at Belmont—I could probably get rides there. I am going to miss Champion, though."

"We will take excellent care of him," Jamal assured her. "Kalim will be devoted to him, I promise you."

"I know," Cindy said.

When she called the airport to get flight information, Cindy learned there was a flight leaving first thing in the morning for New York.

Before she packed, she went to Champion's stall. The big stallion was dozing, and he blinked sleepily when she let herself into his stall. She gave the big horse a hug, dismayed to realize that she was crying.

"I'm going to miss you so much, big guy," she said into his silky mane. "You be good for Kalim, okay?"

She ran her hand down his shoulder, trying to memorize the feel of his coat, and pressed her cheek to his nose, feeling the velvety softness of his muzzle. "You'll be fine here, I know it."

Champion shoved his nose at her, and Cindy bit back a sob. "I don't want to leave you," she said. "But I know you'll be treated well here for the rest of your life. I have to go, boy. I just have to."

"I will take good care of Champion," Kalim said from behind her.

Cindy spun around, swiping at her damp face. "I know you will," she said.

"I will miss you, Cindy," Kalim said sadly.

"I'll miss you, too," she said, giving him a quick hug before she hurried from the barn, leaving Kalim with Champion.

She whipped through her room, throwing her few possessions into her suitcase.

"What are you doing?"

She spun around to see Ben standing in the open doorway of the room.

"I'm going home," she said, surprised at how good that sounded.

"What about Champion?" Ben asked.

"He has Kalim," Cindy said. "Champion will be

fine." She pushed the last of her clothes into her suit-case and snapped the lock shut.

"You're running away," Ben said accusingly.

"I am not," Cindy said. "I just need to be some-where where women are allowed to ride and to win. But you wouldn't understand. You think women have no business on the track."

Ben's eyes widened. "You were listening to my father and me?"

"I heard enough," she said.

"But you misunderstood," Ben exclaimed, catching at her arm.

"There's nothing you can say that would change my mind," she said. "I can't spend my life waiting for someone to give me a chance. I have to go, Ben." She saw in his face that he accepted the finality of her words.

When he turned to leave, his shoulders sagged and his head was bowed. Cindy wanted to stop him, but she remembered his betrayal and hardened her heart. She could never trust Ben again, and she couldn't live happily while being denied the one thing she had worked so hard for, the one thing she lived to do. She was a jockey, and she was going someplace where she would have a chance to prove herself. Then she would go back to Kentucky a winner.

She lay on the bed and tried to rest, but she was

wide-awake. Now that she had decided to leave, she wanted to go immediately. She found her diary in the suitcase and began to write.

This is it. I am leaving Dubai and going home. I will never see Ben, or Champion, again. I should have known Ben and I would never be more than friends. He isn't Prince Charming, and I am definitely not Cinderella. I'm just going to dedicate myself to racing. Maybe I'll get a chance to race against an al-Rihani horse someday, and win.

16

CINDY SLAMMED THE DIARY SHUT, FEELING THE HEAT CLIMB her face. She looked around the Whitebrook barn, feeling as though she had just been transported through time and space, jumping twelve years and thousands of miles from Dubai to Kentucky. The colt in the stall behind her shifted his weight, and Cindy turned, sure for a second that she was seeing Champion, not Star, in the stall. She shook her head, trying to clear it, and when she looked at the horse again, Star gazed back at her with soft, dark eyes.

She rubbed his poll and held up the diary. Star sniffed at the cover. "I must have left this sitting on the cot when I grabbed my suitcase," she said. When she thought back on the last twelve years, she had done exactly what she had written. She had dedicated herself to racing and made horses her life.

She cringed, thinking about the diary sitting there in her empty quarters in the al-Rihanis' stable. There was only one reason Ben would have made such a point of returning it to her. He must have read it. Cindy closed her eyes and leaned back against Star's stall. She hoped he realized all those entries were the writings of a much younger Cindy. The adult she had become was much less naive.

"How embarrassing," she muttered to herself, pressing her hands to her face.

"What's embarrassing?"

Cindy turned to see Christina strolling down the aisle, still dressed in her school clothes. Her boyfriend, Parker Townsend, was at her side. Parker gave Cindy a friendly smile, but his attention was focused on Christina.

"Nothing," Cindy said quickly. "I'm just talking to myself. That's what happens when you get old, you know."

"Right," Christina drawled. She leaned over the stall door to give Star's nose a stroke. "But I talk to myself sometimes, too," she said. "And I'm not old."

Parker smiled fondly at her. "No, just crazy," he told her with a laugh. Christina poked him in the ribs.

Cindy could see in Parker's face that he adored Christina, who smiled up at him lovingly. She thought about what she and Ben might have had, and she wished things could have been different. But there was no use wishing for things that could never have worked. She was much better off the way things were now.

"Are you all right?" Parker asked Cindy, giving her a quizzical look.

"Fine," Cindy said quickly. "Why do you ask?"

"You have the strangest look on your face," Parker said.

"I was just thinking that the two of you make a cute couple," Cindy said.

Christina gave her a wide-eyed look. "I've never heard you use the word *cute* before," she said.

Cindy curled her lip. "And if you tell anyone I used it, I'll deny it," she said quickly. "Don't you two have a movie to go to or something? Star and I were just having a nice chat."

"We're going," Christina said good-humoredly, pausing to plant another kiss on Star's nose. "But be careful what you say to Star, Cindy. He tells me everything."

Cindy watched Christina and Parker leave the barn, and then she turned to Star. "You won't tell her everything, will you?" she asked, rubbing his forehead.

Star gazed at her with gentle, liquid eyes.

"No," Cindy said. "I know I can trust you with a secret." She glanced down at the diary she was still gripping, and then looked back at Star. "I think I'm still in love with Ben after all these years. Isn't that the craziest thing you ever heard?"

Star snorted softly, and Cindy nodded. "I thought so, too," she said. "Crazy, just crazy." She smoothed the colt's forelock. "And nothing will ever come of it. It's way too late for that. But you know what, Star?"

The colt gazed at her steadily.

"The time I spent in Dubai was tough, but I've been through worse since. And I've survived." She flexed her shoulder and smiled at the colt. "I'm going to get through this. Even if I can't ever race again, I'm going to be okay."

She started to put the old diary back in the bag. "You know," she said, frowning at the cover, "I started a new diary when I got to New York. It must be buried somewhere in all the junk in my apartment." She winced, thinking of the mess in her apartment.

She gave Star one last pat. "I guess it's time I went back to New York and figured out what I'm going to do next," she said. She tucked the bag under her arm and headed back to the McLeans' cottage to plan her trip to New York.

MARY NEWHALL ANDERSON spent her childhood exploring back roads and trails on horseback with her best friend. She now lives with her husband, her horse-crazy daughter, Danielle, and five horses on Washington State's Olympic Peninsula. Mary has published novels and short stories for both adults and young adults.